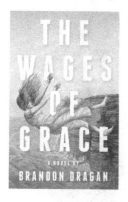

Thierry Laroque, war hero and retired mechanic in rural Tennessee, would like nothing more than to live out his days in peace and quiet, but a dark secret buried in the distant past continues to haunt him. When his Wall Street power-broker brother-the person he blames for the loss of his one true love-shows up destitute at his door after decades of estrangement, Thierry comes face to face with the ghosts of a life frozen in time.

Epic in scope yet intimate in detail, *The Wages of Grace* asks the universally human questions of not only whether healing and forgiveness are possible, but ultimately, are they worth the cost?

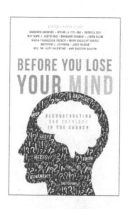

So, you're deconstructing your faith? It can be painful. It can be scary. But the good news is that you're not alone, and you don't have to lose your mind in the process.

This book was created to give you hope for your journey from faith to doubt and back again. To a place where embracing mystery is what true faith is all about. Because the opposite of faith isn't doubt. It's *certainty*.

*Before You Lose Your Mind* features contributions from Brandon Andress, Michelle Collins, Derrick Day, Brandon Dragan, Matthew J. Distefano, Jason Elam, Maria Francesca French, Keith Giles, Mark Karris, Matthew J. Korpman, Josh Roggie, Rev. Dr. Katy Valentine, and Skeeter Wilson.

*The Resurrection of Jesse Barrow*
2022 Copyright © Brandon Dragan

*Advokat*
2021 Copyright © Brandon Dragan
First Publication by the *American Bar Association Journal*, November 2021

*Cast No Shadow*
2018 Copyright © Brandon Dragan

*Camino Real*
2017 Copyright © Brandon Dragan

*Open Hands*
2021 Copyright © Brandon Dragan

*Isolated and Unheard: Can Restorative Justice Practices Offer Better Outcomes for Both Offenders and Victims of Crime than Current Retributive Sentencing Policy?*
2021 Copyright © Brandon Dragan

1st Edition

Cover design and layout by Rafael Polendo (polendo.net)
Cover and interior illustrations by Derik Hobbs (derikhobbsillustration.com)

ISBN 978-1-957007-10-6

This volume is printed on acid free paper and meets ANSI Z39.48 standards.
Printed in the United States of America

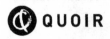 QUOIR

Published by Quoir
Oak Glen, California

www.quoir.com

# THE
# RESURRECTION
## OF
# JESSE BARROW

*A Novella & Collected Works*

## BRANDON DRAGAN

# ACKNOWLEDGMENTS

For my girls, as always.

Thanks to my parents, extended family, friends, and everyone who has given me a chance.

Huge thanks to Rafael Polendo, Matthew Distefano, Derik Hobbs, Elliott Davis, Jamie Jean, Chris Katchucka, Dr. Glen Olsen, Dr. Sandra Hutchins, Donnavon Vasek, Divyesh Gopal, Professors Kristi Arth, Lynn Zehrt, Tory Johnson, Jeffrey Usman, and Lucian Dervan.

# CONTENTS

*Fiction*

# THE RESURRECTION OF JESSE BARROW

## SAUSAGE AND JUSTICE

Folks in these parts like two things most of all: sausage and justice, though I reckon they wouldn't much care to watch how either one is made.

I was born and lived Jesse Edmond Barrow in Percy County, Alabama in a small town called Haywood, just a few miles west of Elba. I was twenty-one years old in 1912. That year I was convicted of the first-degree murder of our Mayor, Archibald Twombly. I turned twenty-two years old the day I'd be the first man put to death by electricity in the bowels of Wetumpka State Penitentiary.

I wrote this, in part, to tell you that I didn't have *nothing* to do with it.

Truth is, they'd never find the bastard who genuinely done it because, well you see ... he didn't do it either.

## THE MORNING OF A MURDER

I awoke with the first rays of the sun as was my custom when I hadn't been drinking the previous evening, although on this occasion I had been, granted, though not nearly to the extent which had most recently been my habit. In the months leading up to this morning, you see, I had experienced something of a downward spiral.

The cause of my recent despair was twofold. Firstly, I had learnt that the singular investment on which any hope of the improvement of my condition in life was predicated, had come to naught. My partner in the failed scheme was none other than Sylvester Twombly, brother of the soon to be late Mayor. Our purpose was to purchase stock in a shipment of cotton bound for Europe, into which I invested every spare cent I'd ever earned and then some. However, my rat bastard partner absconded with our investment and was last seen patronizing a high dollar whorehouse in a low dollar quarter of New Orleans.

Secondly, and post haste, it was discovered that my wife of two years had been unfaithful, though I was oblivious, at that time, of the identity of her clandestine paramour. In the spring of that year Audra, having learned the full extent of my ruination, left me, and moved in with her elderly aunt over in Natchitoches. The week prior to the Mayor's murder I had received divorce papers by dispatch. It was against this backdrop that the charges against me unfurled.

Two nights prior to the murder, and in a particularly thorough state of inebriation, I was observed to have verbally confronted Mayor Twombly outside of McCabe's, the local watering hole. It was the recollection of some several witnesses that the language I directed toward him was incontrovertibly direct and shamefully vulgar. I'm said to have grabbed the Mayor by the lapels of his coat and threatened what might happen were his brother to show his face in Haywood once again. A group of onlookers were described to have physically separated me from the man and sent me stumbling on my way. I have no reason to doubt this accounting of events, though I am not, by virtue of my condition at the time, able to recall them to any meaningful extent.

Late the following evening, I ventured over to the home of Tom Branch, my best friend in life. Tom's wife and three children were already in their beds when I arrived with a bottle of whisky. We sat on the front porch of his home—which consisted of nothing more than an old slave house that, back in those days, might have housed three or four families. The Branches, though, were fortunate enough to have the three rooms all to themselves. Tom and I drank steadily and talked infrequently, as was our established ritual. Having grown up and lived our entire lives on neighboring properties, Tom and I lacked the necessity of sustained conversation in order to feel heard by each other.

Once I arrived home, my sleep was greatly thwarted by bouts of regurgitation which left me feeling devoid of fluids altogether during one of the most humid nights I could recall to recent memory. By morning, however, this condition seemed nothing more than what a strong kettle of coffee and a healthy helping of twist couldn't cure.

I watched the sun come up that day from the porch of my own family's ancestral home. Like my friend Tom's house, mine consisted of three rooms. However, unlike the Branch's modest abode, the house I was raised in had never been intended for more than one family but had been erected and occupied first by my great-grandfather, who was during his life overseer of slaves at Magnolia Hill. My great-grandfather passed the place, along with the occupation, to my grandfather who had earnestly intended to pass both along to my father, though he had been unable to pass down his profession in particular due to a certain *Proclamation* of a particularly meddlesome man of inelegant height and insufferable precepts. Or, at least, that was how my grandfather viewed it.

My father took over the place and a small plot after James Thaxton III allowed his inheritance to lapse into equal parts debt and disrepair. Magnolia Hill was, in essence, sold piecemeal until nothing was left but the manor house itself. As you might imagine, however, fate would eventually force Mr. Thaxton III to sell even the estate's crown jewel, and to none other than the patriarch of the Twombly family.

After Emmet Twombly and his wife Margorie passed into dissolution of the flesh, their eldest son Archibald inherited the house which stands, as the crow flies, less than nine-tenths of a mile from mine.

Speaking of my father, he died when I was but an infant, and I have no honest recollection of him at all. My mother said he was a kinder man than my more severe grandfather before him, and she mourned my father the rest of her life, never taking on so much as a casual lover in the years before her own dissolution. Having reached the age of majority and being without siblings, upon my mother's death the old place fell to me along with a few modest heads of cattle and a hundred dollars or so.

While I was not by any standard a wealthy man, her family was of even lesser means, and it was in this situation that I had induced Audra Harmon into matrimony. Audra, for her part, had seduced me to matrimony with a pair of steely blue eyes and a smile that inferred a wistful mischief that I had then believed to be the product of maidenly lasciviousness that I, particularly, languished to satiate. As it so happened, well ... Back to what happened the day the Mayor was murdered.

Just when I'd finished my daily rituals around the homestead—trimming weeds out of the vegetable beds, feeding the chickens and pigs, and checking my racoon traps—along came my friend Tom.

You done heard what happened up at the house? he asked. I was, at that moment, not paying attention enough to notice the concern in his gaze, though I did from the corner of my eye observe him wipe his brow with the back of his hand.

What house?

The big house.

Oh, *that* house, I answered. Why, what happened—place burn down? It was just then that I did happen to glance up at Tom's face and register the seriousness in his eyes.

Nah, Jesse, he stammered. They're saying the Mayor's gone.

So what?

More than *gone*, Tom continued. They're saying he was *murdered* or something like that.

Murdered? Tom, who's saying that?

It's all about town, he shook his head. His missus woke up this morning and there was a window broken and all sorts of things scattered in his den, like papers and the sort.

Where was he at? I asked, looking up—as Tom was some several inches taller than me—and shielding the sun from my eyes with my hand. My friend only shrugged his shoulders. They didn't find no body? Tom shook his head. Then there ain't no murder, you reckon?

But they took money from his desk drawers and all Mrs. Mayor's jewelry, Tom professed.

Well, there you have it, I said, turning back toward the porch and the pitcher of water on the ledge. Why kill a man when you can have his things?

But the man's *gone*, Jesse, he said in his deep voice, nearly pleading for me to take the situation seriously. He done left without any of his personals—it's just all money and jewelry missing.

I sat on the step and took a hearty swig from the pitcher. Listen, Tom, the Twomblys are the two most conniving, treacherous, and perfidious sons of bitches I've ever known. For all we know, old Archie might have enemies who'd want him dead coming in from the four corners of the earth.

Tom just shook his head nervously. Just then, a rider appeared in the distance down the lane. I'm off, he said abruptly, turning and heading off toward his place through the garden. I took another swig from the pitcher, wiped my mouth and allowed my eyes to follow him into the distance, his sturdy frame all shoulders as he ducked into the brush between our homes. At that moment, the rider had arrived at my doorstep from the opposite direction.

Morning, Lester, I called from my seated position.

Morning, Jesse, the deputy replied. In a small town—or hell, a small county for that matter—you grew up knowing everyone.

I hear there's some trouble up at the house, I said.

You could call it that, Lester Colm answered from atop a brown Appaloosa. You hear anything during the night?

Nothing but the sounds of my insides coming out.

Drink or you sick? Lester inquired, turning his head to spit toward the road.

Drink, I answered.

You didn't hear nothing, then? Nobody came through here or nothing?

I shook my head, my elbows propped behind me on the top of three porch steps. Was quiet out here, I answered.

How late you stay up drinking?

Me and Tom was at his place until, oh, bout two-thirty, I reckon.

You and *Tom*?

As per our usual.

Lester nodded and glanced off in the direction of the Branch home. I think Sheriff Nolan's gonna want a word with you.

What for? I asked, spitting into the bushes beside me. I done told you I didn't hear nothing.

Just to get a statement to that effect, I reckon.

I shrugged. He's gonna have to wait—got business to take care of round here today.

Naw, you need to go on down to his office directly, Jesse.

I looked up and saw the most peculiar of looks on Lester's face. He was an ugly somabitch on his best day, but just then, the way his brow was ruffled, and he wouldn't looked me in the eye, gave me a cold shiver.

Alright, Lester, I consented, leaning forward and trying to get a better read on what had changed in his manner. I'll see Nolan directly—just let me change shirts and make a sandwich.

He nodded, still looking off toward the Branch plot, then made a clicking sound with his teeth and was back off toward town.

## THE AFTERNOON OF A MURDER

The center of town was just abuzzing when I got there. Mayor Twombly had been murdered and no one felt safe, apparently, judging from the brazen and liberal displays of arms in the holster and over the shoulder of near every man present. It seemed as if simultaneously one set of horses and wagons moved in every direction while another set blocked the streets in a most inexpedient manner.

I came upon James Amland, a native fellow I'd known since our schoolhouse days. James, who had mostly the appearance of white man, maintained the habit of wearing a set of beads around his neck in the fashion of his Choctaw ancestors on his mother's side. Being that his father was a white man who had landed upon these shores from the distance fiefdoms of Scandinavia, one might be forgiven for believing James Amland to be a bit of an imposter—for James was a white man in social situations in town, and an Indian when it suited him outside of it. His skin in summer was a reddish brown and his hair was black as coal; yet his pale blue eyes would always betray him for what he actually was: a mongrel of mixed race.

These are simply my personal observations, I'll have you know. I always liked James Amland and enjoyed his company. I never did envy the delicate lines he would be forced to walk between cultures. I myself was a mongrel of sorts, the blood of kingdoms and peoples too numerous to count flowing through my blue veins. The only difference between me and James Amland, I suppose, is that my ancestors had managed to fornicate and procreate within the confines of similar skin tones, and there's certainly no virtue in that, in and of itself.

Mr. Amland, I called as I approached on foot. James turned his head over his left shoulder and nodded.

Mr. Barrow, he answered, wad of tobacco occupying one side of his mouth.

What's the news about town?

They say the mayor was murdered, came the terse reply.

That's what I hear, I commented. The old boy looked at me with those lambent eyes and raised his brows. But you don't think so?

He sniffled and scratched at his nose with his forefinger. There ain't no body.

Ain't no body? I asked.

There ain't no body.

We both watched the courthouse in the center of the bustling square, movement and commotion, voices and whispers.

How do they know he was murdered, then?

They don't, answered Amland. They just think it.

*Ain't no body*, I thought to myself. That didn't mean shit. Well, unless by shit, I meant that they just hadn't found it yet.

Well, James, I began, wiping the sweat from my brow and then replacing my hat atop my head. The good Sheriff wants a word with me.

The Sheriff? he asked quizzically.

Mhmm.

You be careful now, Amland drawled, casting his eyes from the chaotic scene before us to the heavens and back. Something don't feel right about all this.

Ain't nothing much been right about this part of the world for quite some time, I chuckled. But I hear you talking, and I'll take it under advisement.

You sound like a politician now, he said, spitting off to the side of the road.

Well hell, James, you don't have to insult me.

A wry smile crept across his lips as he looked to the sky once more.

Well, you be good, I said.

You, too.

In a minute's time I was inside the courthouse, following a single sign that pointed toward the Sheriff's office. Inside that office was Ms. Wynona Mays, a fire-haired young lady in her early twenties. She acted as secretary—and who knows, maybe more—for Sheriff Nolan. She was tall and slender, green-eyed, and freckled. Her father was a sharecropper with a small plot of land on the other side of town from mine. She wasn't much use to him though, I imagine. Wynona's skin was so pale that she couldn't work outside for more than ten minutes, or it would turn the color of her hair and she'd be sick for a week. In fact, the joke was about town that she could appear in two colors: either cotton or tomato. She was pleasant on the eye, though, and appeared to have some wit to her, as well. I hadn't much had the opportunity to speak with her before that afternoon, but always made a point to say hello when I saw her about town.

On a morning as peculiarly troubling as this one, you might expect to see a debutante such as Wynona Mays fainted at her desk or sniffling into a kerchief at the very least. But Wynona Mays was tougher than she looked. At that moment, in fact, I believe the townspeople would have been no worse off had they pinned the gold star on her chest and shuffled Nolan off into early retirement. Maybe he would have finally found the bottom of the barrel he'd been looking for all those years.

But there I stood, watching her fingers fly over that typewriter until that cylinder hit the end of the line. At that point, she'd slam it back into place and keep going, pausing only to take a drag on a cigarette that, when not in use, rested across the rim of a coffee mug like that's where it belonged. Without even looking up to see it was me, Wynona asked, You here to see Nolan?

Yes, ma'am, I answered, holding my hat in my hands.

I reckon Lester Colm went by your place, she stated flatly.

He did, said I.

*Catch-aka, catch-aka, catch-aka, ding.*

Wynona finally looked up.

Well, I'll be damned, she smiled mordantly. Only took the god-damn Mayor getting murdered to get *him* off his ass.

Sounds like Lester, I answered.

She simultaneously stood and peeled that sheet of paper from the grips of the typewriter, then walked toward the back office and opened the door without knocking. From where I stood, I could see Sheriff Nolan with his elbows on his knees, his head in his hands, and a whisky poured to the brim on his desk. He looked up suddenly, his unshaven face paunchy and rufous, surprised by her entrance.

Barrow's here, she called.

Send him in, send him in, he replied, waving one hand while taking hold of the drink in the other.

Wynona nodded toward me and held the door open. As I passed, I couldn't help but get a whiff of neroli and maybe peony about her person—a pleasant smell that made me think of more untroubled days.

That's a fine perfume you're wearing, I remarked. Reminds me of something like what my wife used to wear.

Well, they sell it here in town, was all she said as she let the door close behind me with a thud.

There I stood, hat in hand, facing one of the dumbest men I'd ever meet, though I confess, I did not fully comprehend the chasmous depths of his inanity. And yet, this was the man who would eventually send me to the chair whereby it was the State of Alabama's firm intention that I meet my maker all fried and crispy like.

# THE FIRST INTERVIEW

The current Constitution of the State of Alabama was adopted in 1901. At over 350,000 words, it is more than fifty times the length of the United States Constitution. And on whatever day, in whatever century you might happen to be reading this, chances are it will be both the most amended and the longest constitution still carrying the power of law anywhere in the world.

Alabama's Constitution includes many wonderful benefits for the people, such as the right to trial by jury and the guarantee that one may not be imprisoned simply for being in debt. Navigable waterways are preserved forever as public highways and no soldiers may be quartered in a man's house during times of peace. Additionally, and once more, depending on what time you refer to as the present, the Alabama Constitution may also have outlawed the State's participation in works of public improvement or may have declared that "no child of either race shall be permitted to attend a school of the other race."

Curiously absent, however, at least at the time of my living this tale, was the right for an accused person to have counsel provided him during all stages of custodial interrogation.

Sheriff Nolan was sweating like the outside of a cup of ice, though I imagine his insides were something fouler than a cold drink on a warm summer's afternoon. He nodded his head toward the chair, and I took my seat.

Barrow, he leaned back, his glare fixed blankly on the closed blinds over the window to his right. I can appreciate a man who can appreciate a drink.

I'm glad for that, sir, I replied.

As much as a man like you might appreciate a strong drink—or hell, even a few of them—I ain't ever known you to be much of a troublemaker.

No sir, Sheriff—I tend to rather enjoy the blessings of peace and tranquility.

I ain't ever as much as seen you in the drunk tank, he slobbered, taking another shot down the hatch. For a moment it seemed he attempted to look at me, but his gaze was caught over my left eyebrow on the wall behind me. I recall this tidbit specifically because I turned around over my left shoulder, tracing his eyes to see if someone had entered the room behind me. Overall, I'd say you're a pretty decent fella, all things considered.

Well, thank you. You, too, Sheriff. I lied.

There is one thing I learned about recently, though, that's bothered me a little bit—

Now, Sheriff Nolan—

He put his hands up all exasperated like and for the first time looked me in the face with his round dull eyes.

All I heard was that you had a few words with Mayor Twombly the night before last down near McCabe's.

My recollection is a little fuzzy on just what was said, but—

Listen, he sat back suddenly, looking off toward the inside of the blinds again. I think a man has a right to criticize a public official to his face in this country. Or at least he ought to have such a right. So, any discourse you might have had—however boisterous—is fine by me, so long as you tell me that it wasn't on matters personal between the two of you.

His choice of words piqued my interest and my suspicion just a bit. How much had the Sheriff actually been informed about what I'd been heard to have said to the Mayor? Was he baiting me here? I watched his bovine face stare at the blinds and thought to myself that, while I certainly shouldn't be baited into admitting anything—*wait a second!* I had nothing to admit! I hadn't hurt a hair on the Mayor's head that evening nor any!

Sheriff Nolan, I began, trying not to sound too defensive. My conversation with Mayor Twombly that evening did touch upon personal grounds, but only by way of his brother.

His brother? Nolan inquired, turning to look at me once more. What's he got to do with anything?

Sheriff, my affairs are an open book and I hold no hidden animosity towards any man, I answered, leaning forward in my chair earnestly. It's no great mystery that Sylvester Twombly purported at one time to be my business partner, then beat a hasty retreat to New Orleans once he had his hands on my investment. It's also no great mystery that my financial ruination contributed much to the dissolution of my marriage, and for those things I do hold Sylvester Twombly accountable. But my brief dalliance in the street with Mayor Archibald Twombly was limited to my relaying to him the depths of my sentiments toward his brother—and nothing else.

Well, Nolan pondered as his eyes drifted up toward the ceiling, isn't that something like a motive to commit a crime against the Mayor?

Are you asking *me*, sir?

He slowly waved a fleshy finger in my direction. Revenge, er, uh … he pondered aloud.

Sheriff Nolan—*Sheriff Nolan*, look at me! His eyes snapped to meet mine. At this moment my elbows were atop his desk. I did not have *anything* to do with the murder of Mayor Twombly. Whatever level of animosity I may have achieved with his brother is a matter between the two of us men. Now, I cannot swear to you before almighty God that I would not cause some level of harm to come to *Sylvester* Twombly on account of what misery he hath wrought in my life, but on my honor, I hold no such grudge against Mayor Archibald Twombly.

Honor's a funny thing, ain't it? He mused, just as a bead of sweat ran its way into his right eye. He twitched his lashes and downed the rest of his drink.

How do you mean, Sheriff?

I mean it's a funny *word*—'aw-nor;' 'aw-ner.' I reckon, the way it's spelt, shouldn't it be pronounced 'hhho-nor?'

I reckon I'd never really thought about it in those terms, Sheriff.

'Ner,' he repeated, then allowing himself a bemused chuckled, placed his empty glass on the desk and swiveled toward me. You strike me as pretty harmless, Barrow. But for my peace of mind, just what was you doing last night?

I was drinking at a friend's house pretty late, I answered. Left there and went directly home and directly to bed.

Sounds like a decent night.

It was.

Your friend would vouch for you?

I'm as sure of that as I am the sun will set this evening.

And you didn't hear anything strange or suspicious during the dark hours of the morning?

Nothing at all.

He patted my folded hands with his sweaty palm and looked me in the eyes. I don't think I'll be needing you for anything. You have a good day and stay out of trouble, Barrow.

Yes sir, and you do the same.

I stood, wiping the outsides of hands on my trousers and turning toward the door. In a moment's time I was back in the perfumed and *catching-ing* presence of Ms. Mays. I tipped my hat in her direction as a I sauntered by. In response, she seemed to slightly lift the tip of the cigarette that dangled from the corner of her mouth. However, just as my hand reached the doorknob to the hall, the Sheriff's voice boomed through the closed office door.

What? Wynona demanded with a puff of white smoke, all the while continuing to type. I turned around, hand still on the door handle. More yelling—mostly inaudible to my ears. Then she turned her eyes toward me. He wants to know the name of your drinking buddy.

Oh, uh, Tom Branch.

So noted, she said, slamming the cylinder back into place. Be good.

Yes, ma'am, I replied, closing the door behind me.

# THE WEEK AFTER MURDER

I did my best to lay low the next few days after that chat with Sheriff Nolan. The town remained aboil of all sorts of rumors and innuendos, though to my ears, none of them had anything to do with me. Naturally, as I had nothing to do with the Mayor's murder, I would have expected nothing different.

Like I said, I just kept my head down and stuck to my working and my drinking. My buddy Tom, on the other hand, was more nervous than a long-tailed cat in a room full of rocking chairs.

You know they always try to pin these things on my kind, he'd stammer.

What are you talking about? I'd ask.

Black folks, he'd say, starting to get a little agitated. Whenever harm comes to a white man that they can't figure it, they just pick out whoever happens to be the black man standing closest to the body.

That's some bullshit, Tom and you know it, I'd answer while taking a long puff on my cigar.

It's some bullshit that you'd even say that, Jesse, he'd repine.

Listen, I ain't here for all that, man.

Tom would just stare out into row after row of cotton in the fields across from my place, owned by somebody different than who owned them ten years ago, who was somebody other than who'd owned them ten years before that, but somehow, they always ended up being worked by the same folks.

Plus, Tom, I'd start back up. They gotta have some kind of *evidence*—they can't just hang you for being black.

Who says, Jesse?

The *law* says, I'd equivocate. This ain't our granddaddies' day and time no more—you ain't three fifths a person like you once was.

He'd look up at me with those round eyes and I couldn't help but think he was halfway pleading for me to shut the hell up and halfway telling me he felt sorry for me. I looked back into my friend's moonlit face, and I started to feel sorry for myself, too. Not sorry that I was in a bad way at all, but sorry for the well of my own ignorance I was just now looking down into—that despite my lifelong friendship with this man, I really hadn't the faintest idea of what it was like to walk for a *minute* in his shoes.

There's a lot of talk about pride in these parts, a lot of talk about honor. Grow up around here and you'll hear about states' rights and carpetbaggers and bummers and don't even get me started on that bastard devil straight out the sixth rung of hades William Tecumseh, I still can't bring myself to say his full name.

I'd learnt about it all. I'd learnt about how a bunch of silk-stocking federals being driven around in their rockaways by men who could barely afford to feed their children looked down on *my* people's way of life—they thought we were simple, primitive dolts that they could push around like an apple cart in Binghamton during the time of year the nights start quicker and you can see your breath in the morning. To hell with your tradition, they'd said; to hell with a way of life we don't understand!

We fought hard, didn't we? We killed a hell of a lot more of them than they did of us. But hell, for every Yank we split in two they just threw four more into the fray. They had three times the number of eligible soldiers than we had, after all. Now tell me, how are you supposed to win like that, year after year? You kill the enemy over and over and they just keep coming back stronger and stronger? And after four years of war making, four years of carving a path of carnage and destruction a thousand miles wide from Picacho Peak to Charleston

Bay, they called *us* the people that didn't care for human life. Raped *our* women and burnt *our* fields. Killed one out of every four men in the State of Alabama and then claimed the moral high ground ... *Imagine the gall.*

And ever since then, they've basked in what some have called the *prize of virtue.* They were on the right side of history—*and so they were*—but they've used it as license to overlook every other evil in their own hearts. It became useful to forget that the 1860 Republican Party platform vowed to safeguard slavery in every place it then existed. Lost to the mists of the past became the fact that Lincoln's own Emancipation Proclamation only abolished slavery in those states who would not agree to rejoin the Union by a January 1863 deadline. Nor would it be convenient to remember that two Northern states rejected the Thirteenth Amendment, and that it wouldn't be ratified in Delaware until a new century had dawned. The truth is, the Yanks of that day managed to carry abolitionism in their left hand and racism in their right.

So sure, they spotted and rooted out the glaring plank in our eye, but they failed to perceive the log in their own. And if you don't believe me, go back, and read what they wrote. It was as if in their relentless pursuit of a moral absolute they had sold their souls along the way. They could project all of what was wrong with the world on the *Other*, and since they imagined they had thus achieved the high ground, they lacked the inducement to walk circumspectly about the wheel of their own lives. Their hatred of sin turned to hatred of the sinner, the love of liberty into lust for blood. Thus, they failed to recognize their own greed, their own hatred, the darkness in their own hearts—either they failed, or worse, they refused.

Never mind how the laborers in their mills are practically slaves themselves, working twelve and fifteen hour days for just enough pay to live in a rat-infested slum and patch the holes in their children's outercoats, while the mill's owner eats caviar, his wife wears diamonds from head to toe, and his son lives in a constant state of dissipation induced by tedium and despair. Never mind the windfalls they'd reaped sending the cotton harvested by the hands of the *Other* off to foreign lands, all the while bloviating in a stream of self-righteous delirium about the evils of the very system which produced the very lifestyle of opulence and vainglory which drove them to depths of barbarity which, by their scale and amplitude alone would have been mythical in any other age, had they not been so well documented in their own. Never mind how their will to purify the nation had corroded their souls, turning their hearts to aggression and the hatred of their fellow man. And after the blood of hundreds of thousands of their sons had been spilled on seas and fields from Norfolk to Pea Ridge, after they had achieved their aims of union and abolition, it seems the only thing the reformer had neglected to reform was himself.

But hell, my life wasn't much different, was it? I didn't own Magnolia Hill before the war and I certainly don't own it now. I still worked long hours in the heat of the sun like my kinfolk before me, though, and perhaps by way of an improvement, I worked for my own sake and I don't have to oversee any human soul but myself and that suited me just fine.

In fact, I'm glad it all happened like it happened, asides from a quarter of a million dead. I didn't ever fancy the idea of slavery, myself. That's not to say I would have had any other options but to participate in it if had I been born in that place during those times, but I can at least hope I wouldn't have done so with much enthusiasm.

But that's not quite true, is it? A man in a position of privilege *always* has a choice … Anyway, the thought of one human owning another always seemed un-American to me, but then again, I suppose the idea has been American a lot longer than I have.

The truth of the matter is, Tom and I grew up friends because there was hardly anyone else around that was boys our age. My grandaddy certainly didn't approve, but he didn't voice much disapproval neither.

It wasn't really until I grew a little that people started taking issue with our friendship. I never understood that much and never cared that much either. Tom was as solid as any person I'd ever met, and I don't mean in terms of physical characteristics. He was honest, he was gentle, and he was more loyal than any friend I've known then or since. We could talk about things when we needed to, and both of us even felt free to raise our voices when we disagreed, but there always remained a base level of respect between us, and I always thought that was how it should be.

But those who did find issue in me bouncing around with a colored boy by choice rarely said so to my face. I always heard it about *downstream*, so-to-speak. It was always whispered disapproval, questions about my mental well-being and such. Some system of honor, eh, when you can't even bring yourself to say something stupid to my face.

So, as I stared into Tom's eyes that evening, I began to wonder where my honor really lied—where the fictions I'd been taught by my own people had become so ingrained in my soul that I couldn't tell them from truth any more. After all, I'd just said to the man's face that his grandaddy was three fifths a person. And no, I didn't mean it like he actually was, but I said the words all the same, as if at some point in time it had been true. The stark reality was, Tom's grandaddy had been treated like far less than that.

*Tom's grandaddy* ... the old man who used to sit on the porch and whittle all kinds of trinkets for the kids around. I remember he gave me a little boat he'd made from a piece of solid wood. Who knows how many hours he'd passed making it.

*Tom's grandaddy* ... the old man who used to smoke a whole hog under the earth every June 19th. He would brew this sauce out of molasses and vinegar that was unlike anything I've ever tasted. Tom still does all that every year, but I don't think it's nearly as good as what his grandaddy did. I don't tell him that, though.

*Tom's grandaddy* ... the old man who jumped in the pond with us one time and we all thought he'd drowned because he was under for so long. Then he burst up to the surface and shook the water out of his hair like a puppy, laughing all the while. And when he got up and got out of that pond, the back of his shirt pressed up toward his shoulder blades and we could see all his scars from being whipped.

Then there was *my grandaddy* ... the angry old drunk who'd probably put those scars there with his own hand.

Pride?

Honor?

How could a decent man who came from that feel *anything* asides from shame?

But no, Tom and I were alright. Our relationship was perhaps more complex than I'd ever imagined, though I believe he understood far more than I ever would. He remained in a state of unease all that week, in spite of my assurances that he had nothing to fret because he hadn't done anything wrong. Plus, I reminded him that I'd been with him until late that night and would vouch for his whereabouts.

The rumblings in town were that the Mayor had been beaten severely and perhaps, being as they had not yet found a body, killed somewhere away from his home and hid. The people asked, but who would do such a thing? Who would want to hurt Mayor Twombly?

Folks would stop or pass by here and there and ask such things and I would laugh at such questions, as I could muster about a dozen men who were not only capable of such a barbaric act, but also retained the motivation. It should have been far from inconceivable, to even a moderate mind, that Mayor Twombly was not quite the beacon of principle and integrity a church going populace might desire in an elected leader. But that's neither here, nor there—the thing that concerned me was the level of disquietude I observed on the faces of those who heard me laugh at those questions. It wouldn't strike me until later that my reaction may have bred suspicion, and that, as it turns out, turned out not to be very helpful.

# THE SEARCH WARRANT

It was that orange-pinkish kind of dusk when Lester Colm showed up at my doorstep with two other deputies with shotguns and six other men with shovels. I watched from the front porch, puffing on a cigar, as they walked up the lane, slow and steady all but Lester. He had a spring in his step, like he'd just learnt some piece of news before anyone else. The six men with shovels were all colored, convicts as I'd come to find out later.

Evening, Lester, I called as the ragtag group approached.

He just glared at me and nodded, put me off a bit. When he got to the top step he stopped, his right leg crooked and his elbow leaned in on his knee. He reached in his pocket and produced a folded scrap of paper.

Search warrant, he said.

For what? I asked.

Your property.

What you searching for?

Anything.

Anything?

Anything.

Well, you done found something already, haven't you? I laughed.

Lester's eyes were cold and unnerved me. I glanced over at the other deputies, and they were kind of smiling to each other, too. The prisoners just stood around, hands on shovels and eyes on the dirt.

What's this all about, Lester?

We're gonna search your property for evidence of murder.

Evidence of murder?

He nodded, then looked off to his right and spit. That's right, Mr. Barrow.

You go through a lot of trouble to get that warrant? I asked.

Sheriff done it, he replied with a shrug of his shoulders. What's it to you?

Y'all could have just asked, I answered. I ain't got nothing to hide.

We'll see about that, he said, standing straight and turning to his crew. Alright boys, you start round back, I'll go through the house.

Have at it, Deputy, I said, leaning back to open the door with one hand.

I just sat where I was while they went at it, and to be honest, I went at it a bit too—and by *it*, I mean the bottle. I knew they wouldn't find nothing because I hadn't done nothing, but having the law go through your belongings and your property is enough to make the steadiest hand tremble. After a period of maybe twenty minutes, Lester Colm walked back out onto my porch.

Find anything like what you was looking for? I asked.

I'll be around back, came the terse answer. You stay put.

I put my hands up. This is my land, I ain't got nowhere else to go.

When it got too dark to work they lit torches. I could hear them digging but didn't bother to ask where or why, until it dawned on me that they might be uprooting my vegetables. From my seat I sprang, slightly unsteady, and walked round to the field out back. And yes, they'd dug up my tomatoes and my okra, my spinach and my cabbage. It wouldn't matter to protest none, though, as at the very moment I might have opened my mouth to do so, I was arrested for murder.

## THE SECOND INTERVIEW

I sat there, shackled to a small table in a musty room in the courthouse basement. Across from me sat the dumbest man I'd ever known. He tapped on the tabletop with a pen and shook his head as if to say, this is bad news.

What? I demanded.

Jesse, I wish you'd have been honest with me, son.

I ain't your son.

Now look, this can go one of two ways, Sheriff Nolan said, leaning back in his chair. You can either cooperate and tell me what you know, or we can do this the hard way.

What do I know about what?

About the murder of Mayor Twombly.

I don't know *anything* about the murder of Mayor Twombly.

I can see you're partial toward the second way of doing things.

Sheriff Nolan, I leaned forward, my eyes pleading, I'm telling you the truth—I don't know a damn thing about what happened to the Mayor.

I think you're lying to me, Jesse.

I sat back and looked toward the heavens, then back down at him.

I don't even understand why you think I know something.

We searched your garden, son.

You tore up my garden is what you did—by the sight of it I lost nearly all my vegetables.

And we found what you put back there under those vegetables.

What are you talking about?

Honestly, it shudders to make me think of you eating those vegetables—or even worse, selling them to God-fearing folks in town.

He was beginning to grow angry.

There's *dirt* under those vegetables, Sheriff, I declared.

Yeah, and we found what was under that dirt, he clenched his teeth.

Are you gonna tell me? Because I certainly don't know.

We found his *bones*, you son of a bitch, he nearly snarled.

For a moment, my jaw went so slack that I couldn't close it even though I was trying. My eyes narrowed at his and I could feel my brows making all sorts of involuntary movements.

Whose bones?

Whose do you think?

I shook my head back and forth, and finally regained the function of my face.

You're telling me you found the Mayor—Mayor Twombly—buried under my vegetable garden?

He nodded while he tapped the tabletop with his pen.

Sheriff, I started to laugh nervously. Sheriff Nolan ...

I've got to say, Barrow, he started slowly. You had the wool pulled over my eyes completely. You're a real snake you know that?

Sheriff Nolan, I—

You looked me dead in the eyes and convinced me you didn't have nothing to do with it.

I don't—I didn't, I stammered.

Then how come the Mayor's bones are buried up under your tomato patch?

Somehow, a little sense crept back into my head.

I need to speak with a lawyer, Sheriff.

The man laughed at me. I know you ain't got the money to pay for one, Jesse, unless you plan to use what you stole from Mayor Twombly's house.

But murder is a, that's a capital offense right?

It sure is, he smiled.

Then I'm entitled to one.

Look around you, son, he said. You see a judge sitting anywhere? You see a box filled with jurors who are gonna decide your fate?

Right here?

Yeah, right here.

I shook my head.

That's right, he started. This ain't a trial just yet. Now sure, the way you're going, you may have some tribulations, but you don't get a lawyer until we have to decide if you get hung.

He wasn't wrong. In fact, it would be more than fifty years until a group of progressive judges on the United States Supreme Court decided out of thin air that the Constitution dictates that you have a 'right to counsel during custodial interrogations.' You see that kind of thing had always existed in some form for the federal government, but we have a system of what's called 'dual sovereignty.' Basically, that means that for the bigger part of our history, the rules that kept a check on the government up in D.C. just flat out didn't apply to the government of whatever state you lived in—those bastards were free to do whatever they wanted. So much for the country you thought you lived in. The point is, in that moment in history, I was *fucked*.

Sheriff, this doesn't even make sense, I started.

I ain't in the mood, Barrow, he growled. It's late and it's my daughter's birthday. Let's get this done now or you're going to be in for a world of hurt.

Sheriff Nolan, my tomato plants were all of six foot tall, weren't they?

Fertilized, no doubt, by the corpse of the mayor, he shuddered.

But Sheriff, hold on, I pled. Are you saying that I dug up my plants, buried a human cadaver, and then replanted those same tomatoes in that same spot?

There you go, trying to twist things up again, he said, putting the pen down gently and balling up his fist.

I just … Sheriff, those plants were healthy—ask Lester! He saw them with his own eyes.

He kept flexing his fist on the table. I'm not gonna let you get away with all that twisting of my words and my evidence again.

You said they found bones, right?

He nodded solemnly, biting the corner of his lower lip.

But, Mayor Twombly just went missing last week, right? I mean, that's not enough time for someone to be buried and be withered away down to just *bones*! They didn't find no flesh? No organs? No hair, no—

*You skinned him*, didn't you?

What?—No!

You done killed the man, and then *skinned him like a animal!* Nolan shouted, pounding the table with his fist. Instinctively, I jumped back as far as my shackles would allow me.

Hell no, Sheriff! I cried. I'm only saying, whatever bones you found buried on my land must have been there way before—

You done fooled me once, Barrow. And I won't be no man's fool twice, I can promise you that.

We went quiet for a long moment. My mind was racing and sweat poured down my face and dripped onto my trousers. The Sheriff kept looking down at his fists as he clenched and unclenched them.

Sheriff Nolan, please, I said, lowering my head to try to catch his gaze. All I'm saying is that it don't make no sense—if the Mayor's been dead a week, but all you found was bones ... that's not long enough for the rest of him to—

He cut me off with his glare. His anger was rising, and I suddenly didn't think it would do much good to keep talking.

Dr. Hadley says the bones found buried in your garden belong to Mayor Twombly. What smart kind of reply do you have to say to that?

Dr. Hadley? I asked. Nolan nodded and smirked. No offense, Sheriff, but did you try to get Dr. Mills to have a look?

I believe one doctor's more than enough, he quipped.

But Dr. Hadley? I leaned in. He's practically blind, Sheriff.

He's got a cataract—he ain't *blind*. Plus, Dr. Hadley is the most experienced doctor in four counties.

Yes, Sheriff, because Dr. Hadley is about a thousand years old. I reckon, when's the last time he even saw a patient?

What's your point, son?—the doctor don't know bones when he sees them?

I was obviously getting nowhere with this line of inquiry. I sat back in my chair and let my head roll back to take in a deep breath. Suddenly, a curious thought struck me:

Sheriff, can I ask, how did you get the search warrant for my place?

What do you mean? Talked to the judge.

No, I'm saying, why would you even think to dig *my* place up? What information were you going off of?

We had a tip, answered Nolan, leaning back and picking his pen up again.

What kind of tip?

The kind of tip that comes from the Good Lord to those who seek to do his will.

I stared blankly. I think my eyes may have narrowed and my head may have swiveled back and forth slightly. I reckon I don't understand, I said.

A *dream*, son, he said with a chuckle.

A *dream*?

Someone came forward who done dreamt that Mayor Twombly's bones were buried up under your garden.

Someone ... *dreamt* it? I asked incredulously.

Said what was left of the Mayor was buried under Jesse Barrow's vegetable patch, and hot damn!—he slapped the table with the palm of his left hand, big vapid, gap-toothed grin from ear to ear—there we found 'em!

I thought for a moment that I might be sick. Who was it, Sheriff?

Who was what?

Who had the dream?

That's my business at the present time, he sneered.

This is bullshit! I got a right to confront my accusers!

41

He made a show of looking all around the room. Still don't see no judge or jury here, do you?

Again, he was right. It would be more than two decades before they reckoned that you had a right to some reasonable time to prepare a defense and half a century before they figured the Constitution required the state to comply with 'pretrial discovery requests from criminal defendants.' Some land of the free.

Sheriff, I don't know what to say to convince you—

You can't convince me, son, he cut in, tapping his pen on the table again. Then, he put the pen down gently once more, sucking on his top row of teeth while he looked at the stout hands he rubbed together in front of him. I will, however, he looked up at me, let you help yourself.

How do you mean? I asked, my voice quivering.

Listen Jesse, I'm convinced you buried the Mayor, he said, leaning back again. Hell, God even sent us a dream to show us he was on your land. But I also think you're not the person who *killed* Mayor Twombly.

You don't?

I don't, replied the Sheriff, scratching his brow with the outside of his thumb. I'm after a bigger fish, you see?

What do I have to do with it, then?

See, my problem is, I don't have any direct evidence, tying this bigger fish to the Mayor's murder … except you.

I don't understand.

You help me fry the bigger fish, and I might be prepared to let whatever happened in your yard after just be bygones. He cracked a fiendish smile, and I caught a whiff of his foul breath.

Sheriff, I don't know what you think I know—

Tell me what you *do* know, then. Tell me what happened the night Mayor Twombly was ambushed in his own house and ended up bones under your vegetable garden.

I was drinking with a friend, I blurted. We stayed up late drinking whisky at his place. About, I don't know, maybe four or so, I went home and went to sleep. That's *all* I know.

Drinking whisky with a friend, eh?

Yes.

How much did you drink?

A bunch, I answered. So much that I wouldn't have been able to *start* a fight with a sober man, much less finish one.

He picked up his pen once more. Is it possible you were so drunk that you don't *remember* what happened?—you don't *remember* being involved in the murder?

*Here's the rub*—either response is incriminating. If I said, hell no!, after just admitting how much I'd had to drink, he might take it as feigning defensiveness, which, to his dense mind, could indicate a guilty conscience. But if I admit that it was *possible* that I didn't remember, I'd essentially be conceding that I might be guilty and not even know it. The only thing I could think to do in the moment was to try to backtrack, to weasel out—even if it meant engaging in some creative fact-telling.

I wasn't *that* drunk, Sheriff, I said.

Oh, you weren't? he chuckled.

I remember walking home, I lied.

Let's say I accept that argument, Nolan said, holding up his hands to show me his palms. Then you'd know you weren't with your friend all night.

Under the stress of the moment, I felt as if I'd been had, but couldn't quite tell how.

I ... Well—

Tom Branch, he pronounced slowly, leaning back in his chair and crossing his arms.

Yeah, that's who I was with.

And then who you *weren't* with.

That's right, maybe about two or ... two or three, I went home and left him there with his family.

Did you see him go to bed?

No.

Did you see him go in the house?

No, I answered. When I walked off he was still on the porch.

You didn't see him after?

No.

So, you don't *know* where he was?

I assumed he was home, where I left him.

But you don't know for sure?

If I wasn't with him, how could I know for—

That was it. He was after Tom, not me. My heart, in one tenth of a second, shot into my throat so far I thought it'd come out my mouth, and then plunged to my toes were I felt as if I'd pass out.

You see, Jesse, Sheriff Nolan began, pernicious grin rising on his lips, I'm in a predicament. The people of Haywood are baying for blood—they want someone to fry over this—speaking of, have you heard about the new execution method they're trying out?

I shook my head, while trying to will my heart back out of my feet and into its cage.

It's a ... 'majestic piece of modern invention,' he beamed. They've already been using it in a bunch of states for twenty years already, and with great success. It's called the *electric chair*. And that's what it does, Jesse, it fries a man with electricity—cooks him like a crappy in hot oil. They're buying one for the great state of Alabama—did you know that?—might even be in use around the time they'd use it on whoever killed Mayor Twombly.

Sheriff, I—

I'm not after *you*, son. I want to fry a different fish.

But Sheriff, Tom is not that kind of man, the kind of man that would hurt another person.

What do you really know about him, though?

What do I know about him? I protested. We've been friends since we were children together!

Oh, Jesse, he sat back and scoffed. You know better than to trust a man like him at his word. Sure, he'll be polite to your face, go along with drinking some whisky with you. But don't think for a moment that big Tom wouldn't snap your neck the moment you weren't of use to him no longer. You don't think having a white friend from a good family would benefit a man like Tom? You don't think he could try to exploit that to his advantage, that you'd vouch for him in such and such a situation?

Tom ain't like that one bit, I stammered.

Let me ask you then, Nolan leaned in, you ever leave Tom alone with your wife?

I don't have a wife.

Let's talk about when you did, he chuckled. You telling me that you would have left Tom Branch alone in your home with dainty little Audra?

When that snake *was* my wife, I wouldn't leave *any* man alone with her, but that's on account of *her* depravity, I answered through gritted teeth.

Listen, now Jesse, don't get upset, he urged, again gesturing as if his open hands might calm me down. I'm offering you an easy choice— and I ain't even gonna give you the Third Degree.

That's right, *the Third Degree*. It would still be twenty-five years before FDR's New-Deal justices decided the Constitution said the police couldn't beat the living hell out of you to force a confession, and they had to do some creative jurispruding to get there. I need you to hear that it took *one hundred and forty-five years* for us to decide that a *confession induced by physical torture at the hands of the state* might not constitute the definition of liberty we thought we'd all agreed upon. And if you haven't read *Brown v. Mississippi*, I'd highly encourage you to do so.

By way of summary, in the mid-1930's those defendants confessed to a murder after several sessions of brutal torture and credible assurances that they'd receive plenty more unless they cooperated. We're talking about the shredding of flesh by leather straps with steel buckles. And I'll remind you this went up to the United States Supreme Court—meaning the Mississippi trial court all the way up through the Mississippi State Supreme Court thought this kind of thing was *fine* and upheld those convictions which were *solely premised* on the confessions of the defendants—they had *no evidence* aside from the words they tore out of the flesh of these men. All this time we bragged about the 'land of the free,' 'rule of law,' 'law and order,' when our law was no different than the NKVD during Stalin's purges. At the same point in history, *we were no different*. Do you see?

But Nolan didn't need to give me 'the Third Degree.' He wouldn't need to tear my flesh from my bones. He only needed to tear me from my friend.

Jesse, you're gonna go down for this, son, he spoke softly, leaning forward. I don't want to see that. I'm offering you an easy way out. You tell me your friend Tom killed the Mayor, and I'll make sure they don't strap you in that chair.

You want me to betray my honor.

*Honor?* Nolan scoffed, sitting back suddenly. We're talking about trading the life of a decent man from a decent family for one negro. I can't see how the choice invokes your honor in the least.

I didn't do nothing, Sheriff, I may have begun to cry at this point. Tom didn't do nothing neither.

Jesse, he shook his head. You think a jury's gonna believe Mayor Twombly's bones buried themselves under your vegetables? He paused while I may have continued to cry. Give me Tom Branch, and you walk out of this place and move on with your life, son.

I think I looked up, looked him in the eye, and told him that I would take my chances in court. I'm sure whatever the manner of my reply had been, he was not happy.

You're gonna fry on behalf of a man who ain't even your friend, he scoffed. Jesse, I thought you had something bright rolling around in that head of yours, but ... so be it.


# THE TRIAL

If I was any kind of a betting man, I'd have bet the family farm that I'd be exonerated, and perhaps that's essentially what I did. If you were a betting person, by this point in my tale, I reckon you'd be willing to gamble almost everything you owned on my conviction. As it turned out, you'd own yourself a little piece of land in Haywood, Alabama.

Two days before trial, the judge appointed Alfred Ellison as my defense attorney. Now, Mr. Ellison was by all accounts a decent man, and may have gone on to become a fine lawyer, but at the time, he'd been sworn into the bar for less than sixty days. On top of his youthful naivete, Mr. Ellison was not a lawyer interested in the least in criminal law, but rather, would make his small fortune in drafting real estate documents and contracts and such.

But at least now I had a lawyer, or so I thought. I can't tell you how many decades it will take for a group of men some might call 'activists in robes' to suddenly determine that not only does the Constitution demand that an accused have access to an attorney, but also that that attorney must actually *do something* which remotely resembles acting like a lawyer. I was not so lucky as to have this ruling in my back pocket with which to march up to the court of appeals.

I have no doubt that Mr. Ellison was well-intentioned when he took, or rather, was forced to take my case. He had one full day with which to prepare my defense and I have no reason to believe that he didn't use that day to do what he could. But he was also a bit of a timid lad back then, who wasn't any more likely to stand up for himself than he was to stand up for me, and such a quality does not bode well for a man whose case is captioned Jesse Edmond Barrow v. the Entire State Government of Alabama and all its People.

The trial itself lasted only a day. The prosecution was rather methodical, first presenting the testimony of Mrs. Twombly herself which, though it ultimately had next to nothing to do with me, set the stage for the rest. Mrs. Twombly testified that she had heard no intruder, alarm, or altercation—she had not even known her husband had left their bed until she was awakened by her maid. She went on to recount how her husband's clothes were strewn all about the bedroom, with recognizable signs of a struggle in the downstairs—vases tipped over, though oddly unbroken, drawers rummaged through. His office windows were open, but again, unbroken, his supplies of cash and documents missing. She did mention that it had been her husband's habit to keep all of the doors and windows on the ground floor locked at night, even in the warmest weather.

Next to take the stand was Lester Colm himself. He testified to walking through the house and observing many of the same things previously recounted by Mrs. Twombly. In perhaps his most superb bit of lawyering during the entire trial, Mr. Ellison cross-examined Mr. Colm about the state of the doors and windows throughout the house at Magnolia Hill. Mr. Colm admitted that no doors had been barged through, no windowpanes shattered. Oddly then, rather than drawing the jurors' attention to these facts demonstrating a lack of forced entry into the home, my lawyer asked Mr. Colm how *he* thought an intruder might have entered. Mr. Colm gave what seemed to me to be a rather rambling, incoherent response that would have required a feat of extraordinary agility and strength—namely, climbing more than halfway up the sixty-five-foot sweetgum out front, sprawling down one of its loftiest offshoots, and then propelling oneself a distance of over ten feet onto the railing of the second-floor balcony directly outside the master bedroom, and all while being unheard by the home's occupants. Looking over at the jurors, however—a veritable coterie of illiteracy, inebriation, and idiocy—made me sink in my seat. Their heads nodded back and forth, and a couple even wagged a finger toward the deputy as if to say, you know, that makes a lot of sense.

The big shocker came next, when the state called the Mayor's younger brother, Sylvester Twombly. I know my head swung around like an owl's the moment they called his name, and sure enough, there he was, tall and lanky like a scarecrow in a field. My blood was pulsing audibly in my head, and while at one minute my rage at the sight of the man seethed deep inside me, I also quivered at the thought of what evidence they thought this scoundrel might bring. And sure enough, it was his evidence that had me in this mess.

Sylvester testified about our business deal, only he neglected to tell the part of how he had stolen my half of the investment. He told the court that we'd lost the money when the cotton we tried to buy had gotten burned up in transit. Next, that lying son of a bitch said that I'd told him I'd kill him or his brother in order to get my money back, whichever of the two I could get my hands on first. He led the jury to believe that this was the reason he'd fled for New Orleans—he was afraid of *me*. Lastly, and most catastrophically, Sylvester Twombly informed the court in great detail that the dream about where to find his brother's remains had been his. According to Sylvester, God himself, through the archangel Michael, had revealed to him that his brother was buried under my tomatoes.

The state then traipsed through a couple witnesses who'd seen me threaten the Mayor outside of McCabe's and lastly, brought on the ancient Dr. Hadley to confirm that the bones found indeed belonged to Mayor Archibald Twombly. It was all devastating, and by this point in time, I was glad I had not wagered my home on the outcome.

Somewhat miraculously, the young and competent Dr. Mills had been in attendance. Once Dr. Hadley stepped down and at which point the state rested its case-in-chief, Dr. Mills approached the bar and was granted permission to address Mr. Ellison. I hardly understood the hushed whispers, gestures, and expressions, but something certainly seemed to have peaked Mr. Ellison's interest. He stood and requested an audience with Judge Hackman, outside the presence of the jury. This request was granted.

Once the jurors were removed, Mr. Ellison requested that Dr. Mills be allowed to testify as a defense expert. Judge Hackman immediately appeared irritated.

We've had one qualified expert testify, Mr. Ellison, he boomed. What could Dr. Mills possibly offer in addition to Dr. Hadley's testimony?

Your honor, my lawyer timidly replied, Dr. Mills observed the bones found on the Barrow property before they were buried, and … Dr. Mills came to a vastly different conclusion than Dr. Hadley, as to the nature of those bones.

This seems like an attempt at stalling, Mr. Ellison.

No, your honor—Dr. Mills is firmly of the belief that the bones belonged to a deer … not a human being.

Mr. Ellison, Judge Hackman scoffed. I realize that you're new to all of this, but I find it nearly unimaginable, and to be plain, quite offensive that the best the defense has to offer is the theory that a man of Dr. Hadley's reputation, experience, and knowledge could possibly confuse human bones with deer bones. It's preposterous!

My lawyer was halfway into his seat when Dr. Mills stood up and spoke.

Your honor, he said with confidence, I would humbly request a moment to clarify with the court the reason for my request to testify on behalf of the defendant.

Judge Hackman rolled his eyes.

Dr. Mills, the judge began with haughty pomposity, I will allow you the courtesy of addressing my court for two minutes, but for the singular reason that you are married to my wife's niece. Now get on with it.

Thank you, your honor, Dr. Mills answered. Judge, I personally observed the bones claimed by Dr. Hadley to be those of Mayor Twombly on the evening they were prepared for the undertaker to take possession. Your honor, the most drastic and definitive proof that these bones did in fact belong to a deer was the shape of the skull. The cranial vault of a human skull is much larger and more bulbous, for instance, than that of not only a deer, but most animals. The skull that I observed displayed orbits at the sides, not at the front, as well as a noticeably large projection of the nasal bones. Additionally, the pelvis was blade-shaped and far too narrow to be that of an adult human male. Significantly, the feet of the skeleton were hoof-shaped—

I believe I've heard enough, Judge Hackman intervened. I cannot comprehend any possible scenario in which the amount of algebraic balderdash you just spewed would not fail to utterly and comprehensively confuse the jury on the facts relevant to this proceeding. I am going to decline to your motion, Mr. Ellison, to certify Dr. Mills as an expert for that reason alone, and out of no disrespect for the knowledge of my wife's learned nephew-in-law.

Judge Hackman! Dr. Mills blurted.

That will be enough, the judge shouted, banging his gavel. I will have order in my courtroom and unless you feel a keen desire to accompany Mr. Barrow down to his jail cell for the evening, I'd *strongly* suggest you find your way back to your office, or out to your home, or anywhere else but seated in my courtroom. Are we clear, Dr. Mills?

To his credit, Dr. Mills stood firm, as if he were actually considering going to jail with me.

Your honor, he said calmly and softly, there's a man's life at stake.

That is why we have courts, and judges, and rules of conduct. Mr. Barrow will be allowed to present a full defense if he so chooses, but *you* will not be a part of it. I do recognize your willingness to serve, Dr. Mills, and commend you for it, but you are dismissed.

Dr. Mills shook his head slowly, then looked down at me, seated at the table to his right. He mouthed the words, I'm sorry, gathered his hat and left.

And that was it. My fate was sealed because my expert witness was too smart.

Now, I know what you're thinking, and you're probably correct, that at some future point in time, the actions of Judge Hackman would be grounds for reversal of my conviction, or at least enough to grant me a new trial. But I suppose at this point, I don't need to tell you how many years it would be until …

Mr. Ellison offered to call Tom Branch in my defense, but I asked him not to. Even though Tom was present for the entire trial—his wife as well—seated in the colored section of the courtroom, and willing to testify on my behalf, for what it was worth, I couldn't drag him into this. There was realistically not much good his testimony could actually do—the only thing his evidence could establish was that I was with him for a *portion* of the night in question, and that certainly wasn't worth putting him in the public eye like that, not to me at least. And as Mr. Ellison was out of other ideas, we presented no evidence.

The jury was out for a total of nineteen minutes before word came that they had reached a verdict. I stood there as they went down the line. Guilty. Guilty. Guilty …

# THE WAITING

In those days, the men in robes didn't think the Sixth Amendment dictated that a poor person had a Constitutional right to an attorney

to appeal their conviction. It would be another fifty years before ...
oh, well, you get the point.

I did my best to take my case up to the court of appeals, but I
wasn't very educated at that time, and apparently missed my deadline
to file. And in those days, things progressed a lot quicker. So, once
they knew that I was all out of options, they set a date and all that was
left was for me to wait.

I didn't think about writing this at the time. I honestly didn't think
it would be of any use. I was resigned to my fate and sincerely felt
that it could not come quick enough. I was so overwhelmed by this
feeling, in fact, that I tried to end my life myself on more than one
occasion, only to have my make-shift noose cut down or my opened
wrists patched just before I bled out. Why'd they do all that? Why go
through all the trouble of healing a man you're gonna turn around and
fry in a couple months' time? Is it not enough to rob of man of his life,
you have to rob him of his dignity, too? But I suppose looking back,
I'm thankful they didn't let me go too early, otherwise, I wouldn't have
received the most curious letter from Ms. Wynona Mays.

On June 15, 1913—just eight days before my scheduled execution—I received her letter, though at the time, it was so truly lacking
in specificity or even context that the only use I could find for it was to
inhale the faint scent of neroli and maybe peony that lingered inside the
envelope. In sum, Ms. Mays alerted me that she was not at all confident
of my guilt, though for reasons she could not, at present, disclose to me.
She wished me to not give up hope and assured me that she intended to
make some inquiries and would contact me again post haste. The days
went by then, and I heard not another word from Ms. Mays. So once
more, as the day approached, I resigned myself to my fate.

I had also received a letter on June 12 from my friend Tom. The
full contents of that letter are too painful for me to recall, but essentially, he'd been refused access to visit me on account of his skin color,
even after he'd made the trip of well over one hundred miles to do

so. He'd simply been turned around at the gate. They told him he had the options of either going back to where he'd come or obtaining permanent residence.

In his letter, he thanked me for taking the position I had before the law and called me the best friend he'd ever known. I wasn't so sure that wasn't more a reflection on the kinds of friends to come in and out of Tom's life than it was on any glowing characteristics of mine. Speaking of best friends, he even offered to confess to the murder himself in order to spare my life. Even though he'd had nothing at all to do with Mayor Twombly's demise, the thought that I should die on account of him caused him all sorts of anguish.

I did reply to Tom the very next day, and assured him that though I was certainly not guilty of the crime for which I'd been convicted, I was not an innocent man by way of my own conscience and should the Good Lord and the People of Alabama decide that I should fricassee in this life for my many sins, well then, my time was simply up. I endeavored to convince Tom that he had much more to lose than a man like me—a man with no wife, no family, and no discernable purpose. Lastly, I apologized to Tom that I'd so misunderstood the world around us … that I'd so ignorantly failed to perceive how different the world he lived in was compared to mine, as if we'd been on separate planets our whole lives, while in reality we'd been separated only by a field and a small thicket. Two men a quarter mile apart by proximity, a universe apart by experience. I wrote that I was very sorry that his granddaddy had suffered so at the hands of mine. And that was all. What else could there be?

In the hall where the dead men were kept—they didn't call it *death row* back in those days—I stayed to myself mostly, though I didn't have much of a choice. There was but one row of cells, so you couldn't see any other human other than when a guard passed. The view out of your cell was a block wall they had intentionally painted gray.

The man in the cell next to me was hung two weeks before my scheduled execution date. He'd apparently killed two store clerks in a botched robbery up in Birmingham. He'd been so loud and taken so long that they caught up to him just two blocks up the street, covered in blood and carrying a sack full of thirteen dollars and a couple bottles of a potion that was claimed to cure cancer, goiter, *and all blood diseases alike*. He didn't have any of those conditions.

What he did have was the body of a robust thirty-year old man and the mind of a seven-year-old child. He was fairly talkative and calm, though obviously dimwitted. Over the course of our conversations, he told me he'd never been with a woman and that his favorite thing to do was play marbles. He said he'd robbed the store because his granny wasn't feeling good, and he said the people told him to take the money. When I asked why he'd killed those folks, he just said he'd heard a bell ringing real loud and they wouldn't make it stop. I'm not sure what all that means.

I asked him one time where he was going after he was hung and he said he was going *home*. I asked him if he meant home like as in heaven and he giggled and said no home to Coalburg where his mama and his granny would have a plate of dumplins out for him. I asked him why he thought he was going there after he was hung and he told me he didn't have nowhere else to go after he'd been punished. In the time leading up to his hanging though, the last couple days I mean, he wouldn't talk to me or anyone else. And as the time drew closer and closer, you would just hear him whimpering and asking for his mama all night long.

I don't know if dawned on him that he wasn't going home or what. I tend to think he just got scared of what hanging would feel like. And as I laid on my cot, listening to that terrified man who didn't even have the sense to know what was coming to him, the thought struck me that there's no excuse for what the man did, the lives he took, but still ... was this the answer to the question? Had we even *asked* the question?

## THE DISSOLUTION OF JESSE BARROW

The morning of June 23 was my birthday, and I was to be put to death by electric chair just twenty-seven minutes after I turned twenty-two years old. At five in the morning, some man in a mask who I'd probably never met in my life would throw a switch that would pass into my body some ungodly current for more than two minutes, which would cause writhing convulsions, bowel failure, and facial contortions too gruesome to be left unhooded for the sake of the poor observers. We wouldn't want anyone to be distraught, after all. At some point, it was theorized, unconsciousness would occur, followed by fatal damage to every internal organ I possessed. It was not out of the realm of possibility that I might burst into flames or that those gathered as witnesses might not hear the audible sounds of my flesh sizzling. Undoubtedly, they would smell it. And at the end of this process, there remained the significant possibility that I might yet be alive. If that were true, the process would simply be repeated until I no longer was. And once the partition of my soul from my charred remains was confirmed by a medical doctor—*could I request Dr. Hadley, I wondered?*—my body would be left in place to cool, as it would be too hot to touch for removal for some time.

Now, somewhere I remembered reading that cruel and unusual punishment was prohibited in our great land, and you can imagine my surprise, after being properly educated about the process by which my life would end, that few if any, considered this process to be either cruel or unusual. The word *humane* drifted in and out of those writings and conversations and lectures. Now, there were literally dozens of hog farmers in the counties surrounding the place of my birth, and though I was still but a relatively young man at the time, I found it curious that not one of them had ever considered butchering a hog in such a *humane* manner. I wondered if it had much to do with tenderness of the meat.

At two o'clock they came to wake me, though I had not slept at all. They offered me a final meal of dumplins, collard greens, and fried chicken. I wondered if my neighbor next door had ever gotten his mama's dumplins. The only thing I consumed was the cup of hot coffee that accompanied it. I could not bring myself to cause that poor chicken to become twice fried on account of residing in my stomach.

I had requested a Baptist minister to consult with but, as in a strange twist of fate none was either willing or available, a Catholic priest was brought from Montgomery. That was just as well, as they're all the same. I did pray and I did confess my sins, and then the father accompanied me in praying the Lord's Prayer. For the first time in my life, I considered the fact that, in imitation of our Lord, we ask that God forgive us *our* sins, instead of asking God to forgive *my* sins. *Our sins* ... as if we sinned them together. As if we had built structures and communities and republics and even secret societies bent upon the clarification of our own interests at any cost upon the blood-soaked foundation of communal sin. It was no longer enough to confess *my* sins, because my participation in the world as I knew it had wed me to something much bigger, and with or without my consent, with or without even my knowledge, I had partaken of and indeed reinforced a framework of systemic iniquity that permeated the very ground under my feet, the very clothing on my back. And so, I prayed, forgive us of *our* sins.

The priest stayed with me as the barber arrived. He shaved my face, my head, and my legs, oddly enough. He was a gentlemanlike older fellow, and he smiled at me with genuine human warmth. Once he was through, I changed clothing one last time and was led out of my cell, two guards in front, the priest and three more guards behind. We walked and walked and walked inside that one gargantuan building for what seemed to me like miles, passing through one locked gate after the next. Finally, a steel door of colossal proportion was swung open, and there it was—a single man's singly purposed invention.

It was a moment before I was jostled into the room, and another before I realized the size of the crowd assembled to witness my extermination. To her everlasting credit, Mrs. Twombly had declined the warden's invitation to attend. On hand, however, were Sheriff Nolan, Lester Colm, and what I was informed were a group of reporters from all over the south, as well as congressmen, their wives, and even a representative of the governor's office. How kind that they'd all come.

I was led by two guards to the chair and was seated, facing my splendid crowd of witnesses. My arms were strapped in first by the wrists, then my legs by leather straps at the ankles. A wet sponge was placed atop my head—beads of water running down my cheeks and into my eyes. Some sort of pads and wires were fixed to my calves. There was some nodding and some gesturing, and then the black hood was placed over my head. I was given my last rites by the priest, and then asked if I had any last words. Our sins. *Our* sins.

Only this, I began. If I were guilty of this crime, is this truly what we would want? And if this is truly what we want … *why?*

Then, the contraption was placed atop my head and fastened so tight under my chin that I struggled to keep my jaw open. I was but seconds from agony hardly conceived of by any in the human race, and I had to suffer thus alone and in the dark.

Jesse Edmond Barrow, the voice of the warden began, you have been convicted by a jury of your peers of the murder of Archibald Twombly, Mayor of Haywood, Alabama, against the peace and dignity of this state, in the year 1912, and have been sentenced to die by electrocution this very morning. At exactly five o'clock, electricity shall be passed through your body until you are dead. May God have mercy on your soul.

When was exactly five o'clock?

I waited, the blood pulsing through my ears, my heart racing in anticipation. I did what I could to control my breathing, to not begin to sob as I felt I might, while the seconds passed, then, the minutes—was it minutes?—it felt like hours. When I inhaled, my mouth sucked toward it the rough fibers of the hood. My fingers trembled and danced against the wooden arms of the chair—could they see it? Were the observers observing the physical manifestations of a dead man's final anxieties? And yet the time dragged on. What in the hell were they waiting for?

Forgive us our sins.

*Our* sins.

Would the throwing of the switch make a sound?

If it did, would I hear it?

When the first charge surged into my being, would I feel it?

What *would* I feel?

If *this* was just seconds, how many seconds would it take for me to slip under?

If *this* was just seconds, would it feel like hours?

Father, forgive us *our* sins.

At that moment in the darkness, I learned that the sound of the switch being thrown to a man in my position sounded like a person yelling *stop*. My body clenched, my hands gripped the chair, and I drew in an audible gasp. But I was not alone in gasping, and I was not on fire, either. My breathing picked up pace and I could hardly control my body as a ruckus told hold of the room—voices and whispers and the sounds of chairs sliding around and yet all was still darkness, all was still anticipation. More hours passed in the span of seconds and the commotion began to reach fever pitch.

What? I cried. What's going on? *What's happening?*

A hand touched my shoulder and I gasped again, my body tensing from head to foot. I heard the priest's voice whispering in my ear: They stopped it; right now, they stopped it.

They … they stopped—? I stammered, sobs racking my living frame.

I don't know if it's for good or what, but someone rushed in to stop it.

It was only then, my sense of sight deprived by the hood clasped over my face, that I perceived that the priest had an accent—maybe Irish?

The man held my hand as I sobbed like a baby. I also may have pissed myself.

But he held my hand.

Forgive us our sins.

Father, forgive us *our* sins.

# THE REPRIEVE

By the grace of God and the industry of Ms. Wynona Mays I was not executed by the State of Alabama on June 23, 1913. I was carried back to my cell, as I lacked the strength or ability to walk, and was left by myself for a period of an hour. Finally, at long last, they brought Father McLean back to me.

I'm not a legal expert, he explained. I can't make any promises and I'm wary of getting your hopes up, but it appears as though the charges against you may be dismissed.

Dismissed?

It may be a few days, or weeks yet, but it seems that your friend Ms. Mays has performed a miracle on your behalf.

She's not my … she's … *What*?

I'm sorry that I don't know the details, he lilted, patting my hand with his. But I'm here for you child—they've told me I can stay as long as you'd like me to.

I may have leaned forward and wept into the man's chest, his arms around me like a father.

It was weeks—*three weeks, four days, and six hours to be exact*—but like Father McLean had announced, the charges against me were indeed dismissed. And as it turned out, I owed as much to my friend Tom as I did to anyone else.

A week before Tom mailed his letter to me, a cousin of his named Emmeline who cleaned house and served for Daniel Frederick Corliss, a plantation owner over in Brantley, had stopped by Tom's to recount a strange conversation, a part of which she'd overheard, between Mr. Corliss and my accuser, Sylvester Twombly. Now I had met Emmeline on a few occasions, and though I wouldn't reckon that we were well acquainted, she was aware of my current circumstance and her cousin's heartfelt belief that I was innocent. Emmeline recounted to Tom that the two men were laughing over something as she entered the room with their slices of pie, and that Sylvester Twombly then remarked that he'd heard from the former Mrs. Barrow and that all of his accounts would soon be settled. Being curious as to what accounts my ex-wife could possibly settle on behalf of Sylvester Twombly, Emmeline did well to hover about the room inconspicuously, and to further over-hear that Sylvester was, *by arrangement*, to take over possession of Magnolia Hill.

Tom rightly thought this mention of my Audra was peculiar, and he began to wonder if in order to see me suffer, she and Sylvester had not conspired to have me convicted of the Mayor's murder. After all, who would be believed—even by that vacuous halfwit of a Sheriff—that bones might be found on my property after a *dream*, except one who was respected, at least on account of his family's eminence, in the community? And was that the solution, then, that Audra had wanted a divorce and the two of them had split our investment in order to humiliate me and leave me not only a pauper but a dead man?

In fact, Tom was so bothered by this that he began to stew on it over the next days and even considered writing to Audra for an explanation—though he again, rightly, considered that she would not deign to make a reply. Not knowing what else to do then, Tom began showing up at Sheriff Nolan's office, requesting an audience. He was refused day after day, but again and again walked to town in the hope of being heard.

Finally, when Ms. Wynona Mays finally grew tired of Tom's incessant presence, she asked if she could pass along a message. Tom recounted to her what he'd learned from Emmeline, and at once, Ms. Mays stopped typing and looked up at him.

You said *Sylvester* Twombly is taking over Magnolia Hill? she asked.

By arrangement, replied Tom.

By *arrangement*? Ms. Mays mused, looking over toward the blinds out of the corner of her eye.

Yes, ma'am.

Then her eyes fell back to her typewriter and her fingers began to fly once more.

Let me look into it, she said before she picked her cigarette up off her coffee mug with her lips alone.

Thank you, Ms. Mays, Tom answered. May I check back in with you in a couple days?

She nodded her reply, puffing smoke out of the side of her mouth.

That afternoon, she called over to the office of my attorney, Mr. Ellison.

The *will*?

Yes, sir, she answered. Would a copy be kept?

Typically, not, Mr. Ellison replied. Not in a public office of any kind.

Is there a way to find out who drafted it?

Well, I'm sure it would have been my uncle, the lawyer answered. He and Emmett Twombly were close for years.

Did your uncle keep copies of wills that he drafted?

For most folks, no. But for a man with an estate like Emmett Twombly, I'm sure he would have.

Any chance you would know where that copy might be?

After my uncle passed they packed his papers up in some chests, answered Mr. Ellison. I'm sure Aunt Ginny's got them up in the attic somewhere.

Any chance you'd be able to locate those?

Ms. Mays, he hesitated, there'd be an *awful lot* to dig through. I mean, my uncle practiced law for thirty-five years, and—

Would Aunt Ginny allow *me* permission to check?

I'm sure she would, but—what is this all in reference to?

Wynona paused and considered her answer for a moment. I'm looking into a possible criminal conspiracy.

A conspiracy involving Emmett Twombly? Mr. Ellison asked incredulously.

No, no, she replied. But his will may shed some light on things.

Well, sure, he demurred. When would you like to—

How about right now?

And within twenty minutes, Ms. Wynona Mays was in the dusty, sweltering attic of Aunt Ginny's home, looking through chest after chest of Mr. Ellison's late uncle's papers. Each afternoon, once her work was finished, Ms. Mays would venture over and Aunt Ginny would open the door for her, even though she wasn't having much luck in her search. In fact, Ms. Mays wouldn't find what she was looking for until four whole days had passed. And by a fortuitous stroke of fortune, there were two wills in the same envelope—one that belonged to Emmett Twombly and one belonging to his eldest son, Archibald.

# THE WILLS

W hat *language* is this written in? she adjured.

Mr. Ellison chuckled as he began to be sort through the papers.

The language of *property*, Ms. Mays, he answered.

Is it based on Latin or something?

It's based on a thousand years of common law error, is what it's based on, Mr. Ellison answered, looking down his nose through his spectacles. Sure enough, the late Mr. Twombly—Emmett, that is, the daddy—left the entire estate to Archibald. It even specifically says he didn't want to split the land up, what remained of it.

And nothing to Sylvester?

No land, but Sylvester was surely to be taken to care of—three thousand dollars, plus some livestock from the looks of it. I've seen second sons come away with far less.

What about Archibald's will? Ms. Mays demanded.

Let's take a look see, said the lawyer, shifting papers from his hands to the desk and vice versa. Passing from Archibald Twombly in fee simple to Vernon Twombly and his heirs.

So from father to son again?

That's what it looks likes, Ms. Mays, answered Mr. Ellison.

By this will, Magnolia Hill belongs to Vernon Twombly, Archibald's only son?

That's correct.

How does it end up in Sylvester's hands, then? Ms. Mays mused.

Vernon is up in Tuscaloosa, isn't he?

At the university, yeah.

Well, since he's reached majority, he could have agreed to deed it over to his uncle, I suppose. Maybe Sylvester paid for it out of his own inheritance.

You think the boy would give up his own inheritance just like that? And put his mama out of her house on top of it? Ms. Mays interrogated. The lawyer shrugged his shoulders. Don't make no sense, she added.

You could check with the register of deeds' office to see if anything's been filed, Mr. Ellison offered.

I think I'll do that, she said. But *where*—in Tuscaloosa?

No right here, across from your office in the courthouse, he laughed. Even if the deed was executed up in Tuscaloosa, it would have to be registered here in Percy County.

And without another word the lawyer was alone in his office.

# THE DEED

Silas Mason became the Register of Deeds in Percy County, Alabama, the same month that Dr. Hadley graduated medical school. Mr. Mason was a slight man with a full head of white hair and mottled hands who generally moved at the pace that grass grows. He'd had no recollection of any deed to Magnolia Hill being registered with his office for decades—and he was positive that had one been filed recently, he would have remembered it, the house being one of the largest and most distinguished in the county, after all. When kindly asked by Ms. Mays if he might be willing to check, Mr. Mason informed her that he'd be happy to, but that it might take some time, as his eyes were not as good as they once were. Ms. Mays thanked him, telling him that she would check back late that afternoon.

She spent the workday much preoccupied, which was, as we know, certainly not how she typically operated. Sheriff Nolan barked out orders that she hardly heard, and Lester Colm reckoned he was making progress with her because she didn't verbally chase him from the room in a tirade of sarcasm and exasperation. She caught herself checking the clock every hour to see that the hands had moved but five minutes. When the time finally came, she grabbed her things and rushed down the hall to Mr. Mason's office. To her horror, the door was closed and further, was locked. Then, however, just as a four-letter word was slipping between her lips, she saw an envelope with her name written on it in the basket next to the door.

Greedily opening it, she found in her hands the instrument deeding Magnolia Hill from Mayor Archibald Twombly to his brother Sylvester Twombly. In another second, she was sprinting down the street towards the office of Mr. Ellison. She knocked furiously, and he somewhat hesitantly opened it after a moment's time. She held up the folded deed as if it were an ancient scroll proving that humankind had been planted here by Martians. Mr. Ellison took it from her gently—as if it were, indeed, frail papyrus from a bygone age—and motioned her inside.

Being that his office doubled as his home and as he had already started cooking dinner, he invited her into the kitchen where she was immediately encompassed by the smell of bacon in the frying pan.

I'm having breakfast for dinner, he chuckled, handing the deed back to her after glancing at it briefly. Would you like some eggs?

Sure, she answered, her voice half anticipation to continue unwrapping the meaning of the Magnolia Deed, and half sheepishness, her face blushing slightly. Mr. Ellison was, after all, a couple years older than her, single, and the sight of him was certainly not disagreeable. At the moment, however, they were both on a more practical mission.

The lawyer cracked a few more eggs into the pan and flipped the bacon while asking, When does it say it was executed?

September twelve of last year, replied Wynona, holding the deed open in two hands.

September twelve? he asked over his shoulder. She just nodded her head and made some kind of sound, still searching the document over for new information to take in. After a moment of silence, but for the sound of breakfast frying, Mr. Ellison stated, That's exactly a month after his death.

I think you're right, she said, looking up from the document.

I know I'm right, he nodded.

What does that mean?

It could be forged, proposed the lawyer.

This signature is dead on, Ms. Mays rebutted. I supposed it could have been copied somehow, but I saw Mayor Twombly's signature on papers come across my desk a dozen times a day while he was living.

I would say it was *carefully* forged, then, Mr. Ellison asserted. Could have been copied from an existing document—like you said, there were lots of things the Mayor would have to sign on a daily basis, so a lot of those documents are out there. Where was the deed executed?

Where would I find that? Ms. Mays asked, her eyes poring over the paper.

It should be stamped by a public notary, answered Mr. Ellison. Look to see where he's commissioned?

Natchitoches Parish, she said, looking up to see that he had turned around from the stove.

Natchitoches? Mr. Ellison repeated, his eyes falling from hers and darting around the floor at his feet. Louisiana?

Audra went to Natchitoches, Wynona said, their eyes locking once more as both of them nodded in shared understanding. Do you think she could have forged this deed as some kind of ... *payment* for Sylvester's testimony against Jesse?

That certainly doesn't seem out of the realm of possibility, Mr. Ellison responded thoughtfully. It was about that time that he turned back to the stove, flipped the food one last time, and then plated it. He handed one to Ms. Mays and then gestured her toward the small table and set of chairs in the corner of the room.

Coffee? Mr. Ellison asked as she sat down. I should have asked earlier, but my mind was occupied.

That'd be lovely, Ms. Mays answered, with a little more drawl than usual.

I drink coffee all day, the host remarked as he poured her cup.

I usually don't, but I certainly could, replied Wynona.

Milk? Sugar?

Just like this is nice.

The two sat together and ate bacon and eggs and drank coffee at six in the evening. Long into the darker hours, they formed a plan to draw out the former Mrs. Barrow, viper that she was, and get to the bottom of the arrangement between her and the Mayor's younger brother. I cannot tell you for certain that anything else happened that evening between the two of them, for they remained rather tight-lipped about it when pressed, but you and I can both imagine that a different kind of deed might have been executed that evening as well.


# THE PLAN

*Catch-aka, catch-aka, catch-aka, ding.*
Early the next morning, before the sun's rays had crested over the fields and the dales, Ms. Wynona Mays typed out a letter notifying the former Mrs. Barrow that her husband had been executed and offering sincere condolences. Being the former Mrs. Barrow, she would not have received notification from the state, Ms. Mays and Mr. Ellison had surmised. Additionally, Ms. Mays notified Audra that she, in fact, had remained next of kin to Mr. Barrow at the time of his execution, and that he had unknowingly inherited from a great uncle a substantial plot of land in Percy County, resting partly within the city limits of Haywood. The county, according to the letter from Ms. Mays, had designs on taking the land by eminent domain, which would pay the rightful owner

mere pennies on the dollar of what the land was worth. The acquisition
of the entire plot by the county could be halted, however, by a proclamation from the Mayor of Haywood, and Ms. Mays relayed that she
seemed to recall such a form having been signed by Mayor Archibald
Twombly prior to his death, but that it had, as of yet, not been located
in his office papers. Ms. Mays requested the immediate assistance of
the former Mrs. Barrow in locating this document, which would have
been a preprinted form, the information on the deed already entered,
lacking solely the Mayor's signature, if in fact she desired to inherit the
land which Ms. Mays mused might have been worth upwards of twenty
thousand dollars. Ms. Mays was sure to reemphasize that time was of
the essence, and that any delay in locating the document might see the
property fall into the hands of the county.

Also included in the letter were the true facts that Mayor Archibald
Twombly's office had been left largely undisturbed since his passing.
The town's organizing documents allowed for something akin to a
managing mayor, appointed by the city managers, to stand in until
the next municipal elections were held. In the case of Haywood, land-
owner Ennis Carlton was voted interim mayor, but only accepted
the position on the conditions that he be allowed to operate out of
his farm office and that he not be pressured to run for office when
the election came the following autumn. That being said, Mayor
Twombly's actual office had been largely undisturbed, save for the few
personal belongings his wife had removed.

The plan then, was to allow the former Mrs. Barrow—perhaps with
the aid and assistance of her co-conspirator, Sylvester Twombly—access
to the Mayor's working space, where such a form as was described in
the letter would be subtly planted where even a mildly enthusiastic
scavenger might unearth it. The form would be as described—complete with description of the plot, date of declaration, and all, with
the exception of the glaring omission of the Mayor's signature. Ms.
Audra—or Ms. Audra and Sylvester Twombly—would then be left in

the office alone to sort through the papers, and if they emerged with a signed copy of the letter, their forgery would be plainly revealed and might serve as evidence that they forged the deed conveying Magnolia Hill to the Mayor's younger brother. Being, then, able to put the two co-conspirators under pressure of law, they might then be coerced to turn on each other and fully reveal their plot to frame Jesse Barrow for the murder of Mayor Twombly.

Ms. Mays sent the letter by telegraph that morning and was not in the least surprised to be served with a telegraph within the hour. The former Mrs. Barrow would be on her way to Haywood to assist in the recovery of the imperative document that evening.

The distance between Natchitoches, Louisiana and Haywood, Alabama is nearly five hundred miles, and in the days before rail transit, it might have taken a person more than a week to cover that distance by carriage. Now, given that Haywood, Alabama is roughly ninety miles from the nearest train depot in Montgomery, and that train travel in the southeast at that time was more calculated toward carrying goods than people, it indicated a remarkable level of gumption and determination that Ms. Audra was able to complete the journey in less than four days' time.

But there, at six-thirty in the evening in the Sheriff's office of the courthouse, empty save the presence of Ms. Wynona Mays and the attorney, Mr. Ellison, stood Ms. Audra and Sylvester Twombly, the two travelers eager to be shown into the late Mayor's office in order to commence their search. The fact that she and Sylvester had arrived together, and without the offer of any kind of explanation, further piqued the investigators' interest. Ms. Audra herself seemed to have traversed the much greater distance, and the sweat on her brow and slightly disheveled mien made it obvious that she had not even bothered to freshen upon the completion of her journey.

Despite her unkempt state, Ms. Mays couldn't help but notice that Audra was far prettier than she'd remembered. She mused for a moment about marriages of convenience. Jesse Barrow wasn't ugly by any means, but nevertheless, if he and Ms. Audra had walked into a room of strangers holding hands, more than one curious look would have been directed their way. But he'd had money, or at least more than she did, at the time of their union. So, while perhaps he might have genuinely loved her, Audra hadn't had much choice in the match at all.

Ms. Mays and Mr. Ellison allowed the other pair into the late Mayor's office, unlocking the door and propping it open. The former Mrs. Barrow and the late Mayor's younger brother darted through the open door and without another word began rummaging frantically through Archibald's desk, files, and cabinets. The lawyer and the secretary glanced at each other, then back toward the other pair, delirious in their toil.

Is this it? Is this it? panted Ms. Audra, holding up a pink sheet of printed paper.

Let's see, said Mr. Ellison, feigning genuine inquisitiveness. This is it! You found it, *Mrs*?

Barrow, she pronounced pretentiously. It was stuck to the underside of that folder.

Well done, Mrs. Barrow, Mr. Ellison lauded, before his look and his tone turned rueful. Oh, but I'm sorry ...

What is it? she demanded, an instant before being echoed by Sylvester.

Well, you see, it is not signed after all.

She gripped the Mayor's desk with both hands; her head crestfallen toward its surface.

No, no, Sylvester stammered. My brother, he would have ... he would have had multiple copies of any document he was working on. I'm sure the final, *signed* copy has *got to* be here somewhere!

Yes, we shouldn't give up, should we? Mrs. Barrow declared.

But it is getting rather late, professed Sylvester. Maybe we should ... we should pack up some boxes and sort through them ourselves?

What a wonderful idea, agreed his partner. I could take some files back to my room and search through them more at my leisure. I am awfully knackered by my journey.

The lawyer and the secretary shared another look and then nodded.

As long as the papers all go to one location, I don't see the problem, Ms. Mays said. Pack up what you'd like to go through, and I can have the boxes sent over to your room. Where are you staying?

Oh, that would be wonderful, Ms. Audra drawled. Although we can just load them in the carriage. I'm staying at the Nottingham Hotel.

The Nottingham? That ain't here in town, Ms. Wynona queried.

No, it's over in Andalusia.

Andalusia? That's thirty miles from here!

I didn't want to stay in town, you see ... bad memories and all.

Well, I suppose that's fine. We'll help you load up the boxes.

Once the carriage was loaded, Mrs. Barrow, as she called herself, was off to the Nottingham. Dubiously, she had failed to leave the unsigned pink sheet behind.

As Sylvester mounted his horse—you've got to remember, in places like Haywood, Alabama, it would be several more years before automobiles would be widely used; sure, you'd see them here and there and a few people in town even owned them, but most people were still moving around the old-fashioned way in 1912—Ms. Mays looked down from the steps of the courthouse and said, I hear some congratulations are in order.

What's that? Sylvester asked, turning over his shoulder to see her.

I heard you're the new owner of Magnolia Hill.

His face went ashen, and his lip began to tremble. Oh, well ... he muttered.

You moving in any time soon?

No, ma'am, he answered shakily. I, um, I haven't made any decisions yet, other than, I might let Deidre stay through the year.

Oh, well that's mighty nice of you, Ms. Mays answered. Where's she gonna go off to when you take the place over?

I don't … Deidre will be taken care of. We'll cross that bridge when we come to it, I suppose.

Wynona nodded her head. I'm just amazed that Vernon didn't want the place.

*Vernon*? he sputtered.

Yeah—figured he'd want to take it over, keep it in the family.

Well, I don't … I suppose he … painful memories, is all.

Ms. Mays nodded toward Mr. Ellison. More painful memories, she said.

Well, me too, for that matter, Sylvester answered. I'm thinking I may sell the place once we get Deidre moved out. I don't know if I could stand the thought of living in place where something so horrible happened to my beloved brother.

And where would these bad memories drive you off to?

He shrugged. New Orleans, I reckon. I like the hustle and bustle of that city life. Well, I've got to be off now, I reckon, Sylvester declared, tipping his hat, and riding off at a cantor toward his small house south of town.

Something's wrong about all of this, she muttered.

At that moment, James Amland appeared on horseback from around the corner.

I suppose you may be in need of a tracker, he said.

Excuse me?

There ain't no Nottingham Hotel in Andalusia, Amland stated, spitting into the street. But there is one up in Troy.

Closer to the rail line, she brooded.

He nodded solemnly. I've always had my suspicions about those Twombly brothers and even about that Mrs. Barrow. Old Jesse was always a decent fellow. I hate to see him get a raw deal on account of those folks.

After a few minutes' conversation and preparation, Ms. Mays and Mr. Amland set off north toward Troy, Alabama on horseback, hoping to catch the former Mrs. Barrow in the act.

# THE NIGHT OF THE UNDOING

It was nearly midnight before the pair arrived outside the Nottingham Hotel, a two-story wood-framed house in the Queen Anne style. The place's name was painted in gold lettering on a sign dangling from the eaves. The gallery porch was also two-tiered, featuring posts running presidentially from the top of the step to the roof. A group of three or so men stood on the top level, smoking, seemingly engaged in some sort of trivial conversation. The outside of the place was lit dimly by oil lanterns spaced evenly between each column. A new-model Huselton was parked smartly on the corner and two nearly identical Cartercar Coupes were halted raggedly on the grass, one of them partially obstructing the paving stones which led to the hotel's entrance.

The pair of trackers entered the parlor, empty save scattered glasses on table tops all around the room. The place was almost unnervingly quiet and the heavy fetor of a thousand smoked cigars predominated the senses. Ms. Mays walked over to the counter and peered behind it. A few cubby holes, receipt books, and closed door. She rang the bell and within a few seconds heard a person stirring in the room behind the counter. A moment later, a rugged middle-aged woman emerged, arranging her hair with both hands as she walked.

Only got one room left, she barked, her husky voice pitched in a higher register than one might have expected.

Not sure we'll be needing it, answered Wynona, placing her hands on the oiled countertop. We're looking for someone.

I don't give out information on my guests, came the reply.

Are you the owner?

Sure am, the woman replied, her head unwittingly moving around in a small circle. Loretta Doyle at your service.

Well, Ms. Doyle, started Ms. Mays slowly, looking back in Mr. Amland's direction as he stood statuesque and, perhaps, slightly intimidating just inside the entrance. We're with the Sheriff's office.

No, you ain't, Ms. Doyle answered tersely. I know every deputy, every flatfoot, and every whore in Pike County and I ain't ever seen you in my life, young'un.

We're up from Percy County, and believe a crime is being committed as we stand here in your establishment, Wynona pressed, her natural vexation beginning to surface.

They's plenty of crimes committed in this here hotel all the time, the owner cackled, sending a draught of heavily liquored breath in the direction of Ms. Mays. How you think I know the Sheriff's boys so well?

You must be used to them busting in here, then.

Busting in? Ms. Doyle fleered. They're my best customers!

Listen, Ms. Doyle, Wynona leaned forward. We're looking for a lady who rented a room, we have reason to believe that at this very moment she is in the middle of defrauding one of our ... there's a man who might die if we don't locate this woman immediately!

Honey, Ms. Doyle sauntered, I have heard every legend you could possibly dream up and then some in this place, and you're obviously new here. It's gonna take a more than your little sob story to get what you want.

We'll take the room, said a stone-faced Wynona.

Three dollars, came the calm reply.

*Three dollars?* scoffed Ms. Mays. The going rate for a hotel room in a place like Troy at that time might have been a dollar at most.

Ms. Doyle raised an eyebrow and put her right hand out, palm up. You're paying for the room plus some.

Wynona let her change purse thud on the counter while locking loathsome eyes on the hotel owner. She fished two quarters, and a series of dimes and nickels out which left her with sixty cents on her person. Sliding the pile of coins across the counter, she simply said: Audra Barrow.

Let's check the book and see, Ms. Doyle purred. Once she'd counted the coins, she dropped them in her own change purse, then removed her necklace from over her head and unlocked the cabinet underneath the counter with the key on its end. She put a heavy-looking book, wrapped in leather, on the countertop with a thump. Flipping through the pages, she began to hum a church song under her breath—it was either a church song or a bar song. Sorry, no Barrows a'tall.

Damn it, Wynona pronounced, looking back at Mr. Amland. What if it *was* Andalusia?

James Amland stood still, his hands folded in front of him. Check Twombly, he uttered.

Tu-who? the hotel owner chuckled.

It's a last name, Amland stated flatly. *Twombly*.

Ms. Doyle looked from his direction back at Ms. Mays, smiling pleasantly and holding her right hand out once more.

No, Amland declared, his voice cold as stone. We paid enough.

Such was the firmness in his voice that Ms. Doyle's shoulders softened and the effrontery in her eyes was suddenly replaced by something more timid.

Fine, she said, almost out of breath, her head shaking back and forth quickly. Too-ahm-blee, the man says.

T-W-O, Ms. Mays began spelling.

Yeah, I've got it right here, the Nottingham's proprietor reported, her index finger halfway down the page. Room 202—yep, got it right here. Audra Twombly.

Audra *Twombly*? Ms. Mays blurted out.

At that moment it all made sense—Sylvester had first stolen Jesse's money, then he'd stolen his wife. The two of them wanted Jesse gone altogether and had used the Mayor's murder to conjure a plot that would put the husband out of the picture for good. *Jesse Barrow had been framed.*

Wynona's dexterous mind whirled in circles and kept bumping against one particular thought that was out of place: Audra had legally divorced Jesse—why? Why divorce the man, then turn around and betray him so entirely—particularly after you've gotten all you could out of him? Could he have been that loathsome of a husband, that after you've robbed the man and run away with his primary nemesis in life, you want to see him hang—or *fry*, in this case? Or could it be possible that Audra was simply that conniving, that vindictive, that venomous? Something still felt out of place, and if she'd had another ten minutes or so to ruminate over it, she might have figured it out, but Ms. Mays found herself bolting up the staircase in search of Room 202, Mr. Amland following behind her at a much more placid pace.

Despite the fervid impulse to knock immediately, Ms. Mays decided it would be best to make sure Mr. Amland was right beside her, so she simply put her ear to the door. Though she was not quite sure what she might have expected to hear—perhaps the rapid scrolling of a pen, or the clinking of champagne glasses—the room was devoid of sound as best she could tell. When James Amland finally neared, Wynona knocked hard on the door—once, twice, three times. She called out, doing her best to mimic the owner's shrill sound, apprising the inhabitants that there was an emergency for which they would need to come downstairs. Hearing no response, Ms. Mays was about to knock again when she perceived the sound of rustling behind the door. A moment later the door opened slowly, and the hall lantern shone across the face of the former Mrs. Barrow. She clutched a silk robe around her, the makings of some sort of lacy negligée visible underneath.

What are you doing here? Audra cried, just before she attempted to slam closed the door.

Ms. Mays did well to get her slight frame in the way of it, keeping it propped open long enough for Mr. Amland to do his part to force entry into the room. Over Audra's shoulder, Wynona caught sight of a man in nothing but shorts climbing out the window, white curtains bellowing as he went. She ran to the window and in the dark, witnessed the figure hurl himself over the railing and start to climb down the column.

Quick! she shouted. James, he's getting away!

But Mr. Amland was already halfway down the stairs in hot pursuit.

Sit down and don't you think about moving! Ms. Mays demanded. Audra complied begrudgingly.

You can't just come busting into someone's hotel room in the middle of the night, whined the former Mrs. Barrow. It's against the law or something.

Wynona shook her head and then began to glance around the room. You sure are a huckster, aren't you?

What do you mean?

Giving a false name to the hotel lady downstairs, Ms. Mays said while she began to leaf through some papers on top of the bureau.

I didn't give no false name, retorted Audra.

So, what, you and Sylvester went and got hitched on the fly?

*Sylvester?* Audra repeated, her eyes narrowing.

And here! Here it is! exclaimed Wynona, holding up the fake form she had typed. You forged his signature! I knew it!

Forged *whose* signature? demanded Audra.

At that moment, heavy footsteps approached from the hall and James Amland—matter-of-factly—declared: I got him.

We got both of them! answered Ms. Mays, holding the paper out to show her partner. And then, the man Mr. Amland had by the scruff of the neck looked up and Wynona fainted like she'd seen a ghost.

# THE MORNING IT WAS UNDONE

That's how I imagine that very last part, anyway. She didn't tell it to me quite like that. What did, in fact, occur, was that the couple was brought back to Haywood by citizens arrest and put in the basement of the courthouse under lock and key just as the sun was fixing to rise that next morning. James Amland sat at the base of the stairs to keep watch while Ms. Mays went and fetched my so-called attorney to get his advice. I imagine that Mr. Ellison nearly fainted upon hearing the news, himself.

Even though I still consider his ineptitude and artlessness at my trial to be the most material factor in the very near consummation of my permanent demise, I suppose I should afford him some latitude and perhaps even a measure of forgiveness for his quick thinking in this instance, which assuredly led to the commutation of my sentence. For, rather than reporting directly to the dunderhead with the Sheriff's star the newly uncovered evidence that I had not committed the dreadful murder for which I had been convicted, Mr. Ellison proposed that she immediately and with great haste set off to call upon Edgar Pickens over in Walcott, Alabama, the next town over. Mr. Pickens was, as it was, the only man in the county who owned a functional camera. Fortunately for me, Mr. Pickens was also a personal friend of Mr. Ellison, and additionally, Mr. Pickens owned an automobile.

Within the hour he had arrived at the courthouse in his 1907 Wayne Model N, Ms. Mays, exhausted but resolute, seated next to him. There began to be the morning bustle in the town at that time, and there were a few curious passersby, intrigued by the presence of the shiny motor vehicle parked in the center of our little square. Being that it was still well before nine, Ms. Mays was confident that Sheriff Nolan would not be an impediment as he was, in all probability, still sleeping in his bed. She did wonder, however, about Lester Colm, whose habit it was to make a great showing of his arrival for work, standing about and smoking and nodding at those who walked past while looking down and fixing the deputy's star pinned to his lapel. It was such concern that drove her to grab Mr. Pickens's camera in her bony arms and rush down to the basement where it would be out of sight.

With Ms. Mays and Mr. Amland standing guard, Mr. Pickens photographed the couple in the holding cell, and Mr. Ellison set off for the telegraph office where he sent a two-line message off to the governor's office:

*Do not execute Jesse Barrow.*

*I possess incontrovertible proof of his innocence.*

# THE RESURRECTION OF JESSE BARROW

So, there I sat, hearing all of this for the first time in Mr. Ellison's office. I was two days out of Wetumpka State Penitentiary and one day home in Haywood. Mr. Pickens was kind enough to drive me all the way from the prison gate back to my house. When we arrived, Tom and his whole family were on my porch. He'd been crying. When I got out of that automobile, I ran towards him and he ran towards me. I know not for how long we embraced, but it was for some time.

The next morning, I found myself in Mr. Ellison's office, having the story I just recounted to you recalled to me, but for my first time of hearing. My lawyer, Ms. Mays, and Mr. Amland were all present, though the former was mostly silent. My friend Tom was also in attendance, and was as rapt as I was by the unimaginable events which led to my release. We took a break at precisely this point in the story, and I found myself outside on the front porch, smoking a cigarette with Ms. Mays. She smelled wonderful.

Will you marry me? I asked.

Marry you? she answered.

Yes, Ms. Wynona, said I. I want you to be my wife.

She smiled, holding the cigarette in the corner of her mouth. Jesse Barrow, you may not be a murderer, but I'm not convinced you'd make very good husband material, either.

Of course I would, I pleaded, looking directly at her while she stared out into the road. I owe you my very life—I'd be as loyal and domestic and enterprising as any man on the face of the planet.

Jesse, she said, turning toward me and putting her freckled hand on my arm, don't take this the wrong way, but you're just not my type.

With that, she tossed her smoke to the ground and put out the stub with her boot, nodded, and went back inside. I was left standing there, thinking about what her type might be. It was about then that I surmised that little bit about her and Mr. Ellison being bothered over each other after their dinner of bacon and eggs. Turns out I couldn't have been too far off, as six months later they were married. Good for them.

Back inside, it was still difficult for me to believe what they were telling me, until they showed me the photo Mr. Pickens captured in the basement of the courthouse. There sat my former wife, Audra, next to her new husband: Mayor Archibald Twombly.

As it turned out, Sylvester surely did steal my money, but that was not the cause of the departure of my wife. You see, she had already and apparently for some time been involved with the Mayor, and eventually convinced him to stage his own murder—or at the very least, stage his disappearance—and elope with her in Natchitoches where they would live. So, the morning of his 'murder,' he packed up every spare dollar he had—which amounted to a small fortune—his wife's grandmother's jewels and left for Troy under cover of night in a carriage rented by his brother. My former wife was there already, at the Nottingham, just waiting. From there they did, indeed, travel to the train depot in Montgomery and then on by that method of migration all the way through to Louisiana. While this betrayal was certainly comprehensive, the idea of framing me for murder was not theirs.

Rather, seeing an innocent man lose his life over a murder that never occurred was solely the concoction of Sylvester Twombly.

I had known not the depth of his malice against me, which was, apparently rooted from early days in his disfavor of my friendship with Tom Branch. And I suppose to Sylvester's twisted mind, his ultimate objective was to see Tom suffer the consequences and he thought me to be the kind of person who would have happily given up another man to save his own skin. While I may wish to imagine that I could not possibly be that kind of man, the suspicion haunts me that had Nolan asked me to give up any man other than Tom, I may have acquiesced, rather than face the prospect of execution.

The 'Mayor's' bones were exhumed and sure enough ... they were deer bones. Who knows how long they'd been buried on my family's land?

As for the Sheriff and his Deputy ... I don't suspect they were in on the plot. I just think they were dumb as shit.

Next, then, was the very real deed, truly signed by Archibald Twombly, cheating his former wife, Deidre, out of her home and his own son out of his rightful inheritance. Sylvester paid for the place with what money he'd stolen from me—which wasn't nearly what the estate would have been worth on the market, but Archibald didn't care, as the house was useless to him at that moment. Sylvester did indeed sell Magnolia Hill right out from under his sister-in-law a short time later and used the proceeds to move himself down to New Orleans like he'd always wanted. The shame for Sylvester was that he didn't get to enjoy his new lifestyle for very long, as in March of the following year, he was found in a dark alleyway, his throat having been slit so hard that his head nearly came free from the rest of him.

As for justice for my former wife and her new husband, they were brought up on some charges of fraud and the like, but then were granted bail and fled the state, as might have been expected. I wrote Audra a letter some years later, just to tell her that I had forgiven her for her betrayal, and to apologize for not, perhaps, living up to my potential during our marriage. I never did receive a reply, and as much as I might have pined for a word of amnesty or even understanding, the motivation for my writing the letter was more that the act itself was a reprieve for my own guilty soul.

If you're wondering about justice for me, well ... I received a letter from the governor's office—not even from the governor himself, but from some faceless bureaucrat with a typewriter and a telephone—congratulating me on my freedom. Mr. Ellison thought that an action against the State or against its agents was useless, as it would likely be barred by sovereign immunity. Essentially, then, I was treated as if I was owed nothing after having my head shaved, the substance of my physical being strapped into the death chair and being seconds from extirpation. I was *congratulated*, as if it was my birthday the State wished to celebrate, rather than my last second evasion of being converted into a human lantern.

In the weeks after my release, it seemed that Tom and I reached the identical conclusion that we could no longer live at peace in Haywood, or in Percy County for that matter. Where we differed, in opinion, however, was as to how far from the place of our birth was sufficient. For me, I had not yet given up hope on the State of Alabama, though I did fervently desire to experience life outside of it. Tom and his wife, on the other hand, had decided that being the color they and their children were, they could only achieve a degree of security outside of not only Alabama, but outside of the South altogether. Though their migration speckled the map in more than a few points, it was in Madison, Wisconsin where they would finally settle. In the many years that followed, I would visit them several times.

I went on to serve in the United States Army during the First World War and saw action along the River Marne, but to be frank, not nearly enough to write home about. Having sold my family's abode in Haywood and having no other serious attachments to any place, I lingered in Europe for several years after the end of the conflict. I lived for a time in London, Paris, and even spent a few months in Marseilles. From there, I headed across the Mediterranean and toured Cairo, Jerusalem, and Istanbul before quitting the world at large and arriving back in the United States via steamer which docked in New York. It was in that city that I talked myself into admittance into a local college where I studied business and, by some measure of luck, excelled.

I worked for a man on Wall Street for a couple years but discovered my true calling—thankfully—before the Crash in '29. I had begun buying properties on the cheap, fixing them up, and reselling them at a profit. By the time the Depression came, I was insulated enough to live somewhat comfortably, and while the market for real estate was nonexistent, further pursued a course of study at the school which would eventually become known as Penn State University. More business, but adding to my province of knowledge, some reading of philosophy and some study of the law. It was there in College Park where I met my second wife, Katherine. I no longer drink, but socially, and I do believe this has greatly contributed to our happiness and the longevity of our relationship.

Tom and I stayed in touch until his passing at the age of fifty-seven to cancer. His wife, Mary, is still living as of the time of my writing this, and she and my Katherine have become friends over the years. When I learned he was sick, I got on an airplane that very evening, and arrived at his bedside just minutes before he'd lapse into peace. I held his hand and thanked God that his passing would be much more serene than mine would have been. I think he may have smiled at me, but I'm not positive that he had been sentient to my presence at all. Either way, I was there, and I sobbed in his cousin Emmeline's arms as she sobbed in mine. I cried for months after.

Our children having now grown and settled with spouses everywhere from Baltimore to Denver, Katherine and I settled in a home in the Keys, where she still teaches high school mathematics, and I still dabble in the sale of real estate, though to be candid, I spend most of my time writing or fishing. We've managed to do well, Katherine and me, and through the years have been fortunate to continue to travel the country and the world at our leisure.

Having been all around, having met people of every culture and every color, and having the particular incident I've so thoroughly recounted in this work drifting in the mists of what seems like an altogether different life, I have come to certain conclusions about mankind, wherever you find him. He is loath to change his ways. He is greedy and he is cruel. He is capable of going to remarkable lengths to preserve his own measure of sedative ignorance, rather than facing difficult truths and being obliged to consider a change of his own heart.

But having observed these things, it is likewise remarkably true that we are capable of the most profound kindness, self-sacrifice, and love. It is these qualities that have persuaded me not to give up all hope on humanity. It is these attributes around which I venture that we should fortify our own inner constitutions as well as the societies we endeavor to foster on behalf of our progeny. And it is in building around these things that our children and our children's sons and daughters may experience a world that is more equitable, more honest, and more untroubled. And while we certainly have not all the answers, God forbid that we should continue to flinch from the questions.

So may *our* sins be forgiven, and may we forge ahead and face *our* transgressions with unwavering honesty and steadfast courage. For in this, we may finally achieve a portion of the honor we have so long coveted from the depths of our common being.

— Jesse Edmond Barrow
Marathon, Florida
April 1974

**Fin.**

# ADVOKAT

"I can't do it, Daniela. It runs contrary to everything we raised him to believe."

"*Pero es nuestro hijito*, Pasha," his wife sobbed.

"And he always *will be* our son—never a question there. But that doesn't mean we have to support ... " His voice dropped off. "*Poor choices.*"

Paul Bondar dropped his briefcase to fidget with his necktie in the mirror next to the front door. His stout fingers fumbled over his Windsor knot until he was satisfied, though to his wife's eye, he hadn't improved it at all. She half-sat astride the back of the sofa, her slender fingers knotted around the tissues in her lap. He always marveled at how she just didn't seem to age—her olive-toned skin and raven-colored hair were as radiant and smooth as they had been in her twenties. *His* reflection, on the other hand, looked exactly as one would expect a sixty-one year old to look—especially one who had never quite taken care of himself as he ought. At six-foot-three, and particularly in a custom-tailored suit, he could strike quite a regal figure, forty-two inch waist notwithstanding. But now, glancing from the bride of his youth back to the man with thinning hair and sagging jowls in the mirror, he was equal parts thankful and astounded that he'd managed to keep her all these years.

"Gabriel said he could come for dinner Friday night," she remarked in a much more cheerful tone, her dark eyes swollen and glassy.

Paul glanced at his reflection once more before picking up his Brunello Cucinelli and opening the mission-style door with the wrought iron grille he'd always despised. *It's too modern for the aesthetic of the house,* he'd said. *It's a Second Empire for God's sake, and you're gonna go slap something on the front that looks like it came straight off a bungalow in Long Beach …*

"I think I'm going to be busy that night."

"He's only in town for the—"

The ugly door closed behind him with a click as he stepped out into the swelter of late summer in Memphis.

*It's like breathing hot soup.*

He dabbed at his forehead with a handkerchief while mentally coaxing the car's air conditioning to hit full bore. One eyebrow wrinkled suddenly, and he found himself using the fabric square to pat at his eyes, too.

*Where had the years gone?—the sandy-haired boy fused to his pant leg on the first day of kindergarten? The teenager in the convertible's passenger seat, the two of them singing Stevie Wonder's "Where Were You When I Needed You" at the top of their lungs, while they headed south on the Pacific Coast Highway? What had happened to the young Georgetown graduate he'd been so proud of?*

But it wasn't as if they'd thrown him out into the street—Gabriel was twenty-five and firmly on his own—great job, townhouse in Silver Spring. He wouldn't go hungry, that was true, but his father couldn't see him ever being happy either.

With a deep breath, he put his game face on and in twenty minutes' time was parking his E-class in the second spot outside of Ruiz & Bondar, PLLC, under the shade of a sixty-year-old magnolia.

"Good morning, boss," called Joel Castillo, the firm's receptionist, as Paul walked in.

"Morning," he answered. "You doin' alright, young'un?"

"Yes, sir."

"Any messages?"

"Mr. Ceballos called Friday afternoon about the status of his removal hearing. I put him through to your voicemail," Joel reported. "And Ms. Ruiz asked to see you when you get settled."

"Sure thing," he replied as he moved past the cocobolo reception desk and down the hall toward his team's cluster of rooms. He peeked into his paralegal's dark office and suddenly remembered that she was gone to Belize with her new husband for the week.

After spending a few minutes checking over his calendar and catching up on emails, his law partner knocked and poked her head in.

"Hey, Talia," he called. "*¿Qué onda?*"

"You have a good weekend?" she asked brightly.

"All things considered," Paul replied with a sigh. "How 'bout you?"

"Got out on the lake with Cristian and the kids," Talia replied while sitting on the Fabio leather loveseat perpendicular to his desk.

"Oh that's nice—great weather for it. Tony making any progress on that college application?"

"Don't remind me."

"Hard to believe, isn't it?"

Talia's nod was gilded in melancholy. "One day you're dropping them off at kindergarten, then you blink and you're researching the cost of room and board in one of the most expensive cities in the country."

"He wants to *go* to college—that's a plus."

"But *California*? It's so far."

"It'll be good for him, and it's a damn fine school."

"You're right. I'm awfully proud of him, but still getting used to the idea of being an empty-nester."

"You *ought* to be proud of him—and you'll love it," remarked Paul with a snicker. "Lots of time to argue with your spouse—believe me, I *know*."

"And I need more of that like I need another hole my head," Talia chuckled.

Paul smiled, momentarily looking down to fidget with his tie. "Now, Joel mentioned you wanted to see me about something?"

"Yes," Talia began, leaning back in her seat. "You speak Russian, right?"

"*Russian?*" Paul chuckled. "I haven't for probably, whew, fifteen years?—ever since my babushka passed."

"But you can still converse?"

"I'd be rusty as hell, but … I don't see why not. Why do you ask?"

Something in Talia's glance made him uneasy—like bad news might be coming. "It's a pro bono thing," she hesitated. "I wouldn't normally ask because it's more of a personal favor, but—"

"Don't apologize to me, *mujer*," Paul cut in. "We've been through too much together. What you got?"

"Well, while we were out on the water, Carmela told us about a boy she met in class here at Memphis. They hit it off—in a friendship type way, I mean."

"Okay, go on—how are her classes going, by the way?"

"Really good—she loves it," replied the proud mother. "Anyway, his name is Anzor. He's Russian and here on a student visa."

"Okay," Paul said, turning his favorite Montblanc between his thumb and middle fingers. "He get into trouble?"

"No, it's not exactly about *him*. Apparently he wasn't in class a few days, so Carmela called him—she said it sounded like he was crying. She went over to his place and he was a wreck—told her his brother was *missing*."

"*Missing*? Is his brother in the states?"

"No, the brother's over there," Talia answered with a flick of her head over her shoulder. "A week or so later, the brother calls to tell him he's alive, but won't say where he is or what happened. A few days after that, Anzor gets a call from someone claiming to be part of a humanitarian NGO or something, wanting Anzor to find a lawyer in the U.S. who could help his brother get *out* of Russia."

"That's a bit odd, don't you think?"

Talia shrugged and sucked on her top row of teeth. "When Carmelita told him that her mom was an immigration attorney, he broke down in tears. Naturally, I offered to look into it. The issue is, whoever called from this NGO wants an attorney to talk to Khasan—Anzor's brother—*directly*. Khasan doesn't speak a word of English."

"Well, I'd be glad to talk to him, and try to figure out what's going on. I've gotta be honest though, it sounds pretty fishy at the outset."

"Oh, no question," Talia answered. "Please don't put a lot of time into it, especially if you get the feeling it's some kind of scam. You know what kind of thing comes out of that part of the world."

"Sure do," said Paul. "That's why I haven't done a European case in what, five years now?"

"Well, same—probably longer for me," she said as she ran her forefinger over her lips for a moment, a habit she'd subconsciously fall into any time she lost herself in thought. "I just know my daughter was really concerned and, you know how strong she is, how *proud*"—Paul's eyebrows went up and he nodded slowly—"she *never* asks for help."

"You raised a strong woman, like yourself," Paul said as laid the pen down on his desk. "With a good heart, too."

"Like I said, don't put in a lot of time—"

Paul raised his hands. "I'd be *glad* to check it out—if not for you, then for Carmela."

"Thank you," she said warmly. "And I hope you don't mind, I know you're usually in the office Monday mornings, so I had Anzor set up for them to call you at ten."

"That works. I'm actually in court at eleven, but I can talk on my way over there."

"I'm sorry—I should have looked at your calendar first."

"No big deal," he answered. "It's just a couple bond hearings, and then I'm supposed to be before Judge Hall after lunch for that adjustment of status on Ms. Castillo."

"Oh, is that one working out?"

"Yeah, they just filed in the wrong location when they were pro se—couple errors in how she filled out the docs, too. Should be all worked out, now."

"I'm glad to hear that," Talia replied. "She's such a sweet lady."

"She is," he agreed. "And I think it'll take a big weight off her shoulders having all this over with—her daughter, too."

"Absolutely. Well, thank you again, Paulie," Talia smiled, rising to her feet. "And let me know if you need me for any of that with Khasan."

He spent the next forty minutes replying to emails and paying a few bills. He also gave the internet a cursory check for the latest news coming out of Russia.

Paul was a second generation American. His grandmother had managed to escape Stalin's Ukraine at the Holodomor's height, and found her way to New York, still as a teenager. His father, Semyon was born in Brooklyn a few years later and went on to become a jeweler. Paul's mother was of Colombian heritage, and due to the collision of cultures within the household, he would often joke that English was his third language.

When he was eleven his mother passed away after a savagely short battle with ovarian cancer, and his father moved the family to Memphis. Paul's dad explained that he had a great business opportunity, but Paul had always suspected that his father needed to escape familiar surroundings altogether. Naturally, they brought Paul's babushka—a widow by that time—with them to help care for the three children, the eldest of which was Paul. She would instill in them not only her deep sense of compassion for suffering, but also a strong sense of morality, guided by adherence to the religious faith of her ancestors, one which she might have been tortured for practicing in the place and time of her birth.

Semyon bought a dilapidated jewelry store along Poplar Avenue and turned it into a thriving business. When Paul turned sixteen he became the one person in the shop from whom Elvis Presley would buy jewelry. Paul's sister would keep kindergartner Lisa Marie occupied while the King quizzed a gangly and pimpled high school junior about the three C's and how quickly eighteen karat gold would oxidize. Paul learned a lot about dealing with people and taking pride in his work during those years. In fact, that little shop was the focal point of nearly all of the fond memories Paul had of his father, as Semyon buried himself, along with his grief, in his work. When Semyon passed in 2007, Paul's younger brother took over and was still running the shop.

He looked down at his watch—it was twenty to ten. Paul stood up and gathered his belongings to head downtown. Once he had his car running, he pulled out a legal pad and a pen, in case he needed to take notes during the call from Khasan or whoever it was he'd be speaking with. Sitting at the light at Union and South 2nd Street, his phone rang—an international number.

"Paul Bondar," he answered after a deep breath.

"Hello, Mr. Bondar in Tennessee?" the voice answered in Russian.

"Yes, that's me," he replied, also in Russian.

"My name is Gennady Andrienko," the voice began. It was a timbral baritone, gravelly around the edges. "I am thankful for your willingness to talk about Khasan's situation."

"Of course, Gennady. How can I help?"

"We need to get him out of Russia."

"That's what I've heard," Paul answered.

"I work with a small humanitarian organization," Gennady explained. "There are only three of us, and we have recently begun this group in order to help relocate people in Khasan's circumstances. We are not experts—myself, I am a photographer. But when we began to hear stories about what is happening to people in a particular Russian republic, we had to do *something*. Not only does our government turn a blind eye to what is happening, if anything, they admire it."

"What *is* happening? I checked the Russian news sites and I didn't—"

"I would like for you to hear it from the lips of Khasan himself," Gennady cut in.

"Okay, I understand."

"I will put him on the phone in just a minute, but first, can you tell me about what is the best way to apply for *bezhenets* status?"

"*Bezhenets*?" Paul's mind raced for meaning.

"Yes, what is the process for—"

"Hold on, I don't understand that word—*what* status?"

"Ah," Gennady mused. "In English, maybe *ref-yoo-egg*?"

"*Refugee*," Paul clarified in English.

"Yes, this is it! *Bezhenets—refugee*," he repeated in a thick accent.

"Asking for refugee status," Paul began slowly. "Unfortunately, there's not a lot I can tell you about. As an *attorney*—oh what's the word?—*advokat*—I couldn't really help very much until Khasan was in the United States. My suggestion would be to go to the American consulate—what city is he in?"

"I cannot divulge his location right now, for his safety. But an American consulate is not far."

"You would take him there and apply. There are probably charities in Russia that are better equipped to advise you in that process than I would be."

"But this is an easy process?"

"Easy?" Paul mused. His mind ticked back over how onerous the last few years had been for some of his clients—many of whom legitimately deserved refugee status, but happened to come from the wrong places. The sails of immigration law seemed dependent on the winds of the country's political whims more than many other areas he might have practiced. *At least it never gets dull.* "Maybe the *application* is easy, but it can be difficult to obtain refugee status."

"Is that true?"

"Yes, the United States is particular about what types of refugees we allow into the country," Paul explained. "A person has to fit very narrow criteria."

"I understand," Gennady said, his voice dropping a bit. "Can you speak with Khasan now, and you can maybe see if he meets the criteria?"

"Sure, I'll be glad to talk to him."

By this point, Paul was parked in the garage along South Front Street, the air conditioning still at peak blast. Checking his Rolex, he saw that it was only ten after ten. He put his pad in his lap and grabbed a pen. After a moment, a small voice came on: "Hello?"

"Yes, hello?" Paul answered. "Is this Khasan?"

"Yes."

"Nice to meet you. Did Gennady tell you who I am?"

"Yes."

"I'd like to know a little about your story and maybe see if there is any advice I can give to help you."

Paul could hear labored breathing on the other side of the world, as if the young man was mulling whether he really wanted to recite his story to a stranger. Paul could make out the sound of Gennady's voice, doing his best to encourage Khasan to speak.

"I grew up in the capital city of my republic," he began sheepishly. "I don't know how, but I always knew that I wasn't like the rest of the people in my country."

"Are you a different skin color or religion?"

"No, my difference is maybe not something a person would know only by looking at my face."

*That's a shame*, Paul thought, his mind gearing automatically to the law's preference for "visible sociability" in refugee situations. He was about to ask a question about this when Khasan continued, his voice growing more confident.

"Three months ago, a friend of mine was arrested in connection with selling drugs."

*Drugs? This isn't going well already*, Paul sighed, putting his pen down on the passenger's seat beside him.

"They searched his phone, and no one has seen or heard from him since."

"Is he in prison?"

"I don't know."

"Okay," Paul hesitated. "Khasan, help me understand what this has to do with you."

"It was his phone messages that led them to me."

"Do you sell drugs?"

"No—I cut hair."

Paul scratched his chin with the inside of his thumb and wondered if he might have missed something in translation along the way.

"So what does—"

"I was grabbed outside my shop by four men in masks. They put me in a van and hit me. I was taken to a building somewhere outside of the city and into a dark room in a long hallway. They threw me to the ground and kicked me with their police boots. Then, another man came into the room and forced me into a chair where they tied my hands. He would hit me in the face with a belt—always with a belt or some object, so he wouldn't have to touch me with his hands—and then yell at me, telling me to admit that I was *goluboi*. I denied it, but he kept hitting me with the belt."

"Hold on, *goluboi*?" Paul repeated for elucidation, but Khasan kept on with his story.

"I refused to say until they finally brought a black box into the room. I thought maybe it was a lie-detector test, but from this box they took wires and tied them to the fingertips of both my hands."

*Goluboi*, Paul kept mulling the word over in his mind. *Doesn't that mean blue?*

"When I wouldn't tell them what they wanted, they would turn on the machine, and an electric current would shock me. After a few seconds, which felt like a year, they would turn the box off and hit me again with the belt. Then they threw water on me and turned the machine on again. I don't know how long this lasted, but finally, they stripped off my pants and tied the wires around my private parts. Before they could turn the machine on, I admitted what they wanted to know."

The American sat in stunned silence. Instinctively he checked his watch again, but other than noting that he wasn't yet late for court, didn't even register what time it was.

"Then they took me down the hallway into small room where they left me overnight. The room was empty, except for a hole in the middle for a toilet. There was a plastic bottle of water which I used as a pillow. I couldn't sleep, though, because all through the night I heard screams and yelling on the other side of the wall."

Paul could hear the young man sniffling, and could hear Gennady's soothing voice again.

"The next morning, they took me back to that room—or maybe another that looked just like it, I couldn't tell—and they tied me up and beat me more. This time they asked me to give the names of *others*. The truth is, I hardly know any others, especially not in the republic still, so I was forced between being beaten or giving names of people I knew were innocent. I started giving false names—people who I just made up. I don't know how long it was, but they stopped beating me and led me to a room where there were other men who had been beaten like me. We all just lay on the floor, slick with the blood of twenty of us, all sons of our fathers."

"You were not given access to a lawyer or trial or anything?"

"No," Khasan stated. "I was kept there for more than two weeks. I was beaten every day, sexually assaulted, forced to work—"

In the background, Paul could make out Gennady saying, "Tell him about the work."

"They made me clean the toilets with my shirt or with my underwear, and then forced me to put the clothes back on," Khasan stated. "I cleaned blood from the policemen's boots while they burned me with their cigarettes…"

After a moment of dense silence, Paul asked, "Help me to understand—this is *not* because of drugs?"

"No," came the reply. "It's only because I am *goluboi*."

"Khasan, I still don't understand—isn't *goluboi* a color?"

"I'm sorry, yes," Khasan acknowledged, suddenly perceiving the cloud of ignorance under which Paul had been operating. "It's a slang term now—it means *gay*."

"They did this to you because you're gay?" Paul gasped.

"Yes."

A sudden rush of water filled in behind his eyes, and Paul found himself clenching his teeth.

"They beat you—*tortured* you—only because you're *gay*?"

"Yes."

Paul wrestled the handkerchief from his pants pocket in order to soak up the tears from his cheeks, several of which had dripped onto the silk of his Bolvaint necktie.

"Where I come from," Khasan continued. "The worst shame one can bring on his family is to be goluboi. So when they were done with me, they returned me to my mother and told her that the family should remove their shame."

"What does that mean?"

"To kill me," answered Khasan. "My father is dead, so they called my uncles, but they live far away. I spent those nights awake in my childhood bed, trembling in fear every time a truck came down the street, fearing it might be my uncles or might be the police again. After a couple days, I called my one friend who I knew was like me—he had moved to Moscow before they found out about him. He put me in touch with Gennady."

"Are you safe right now, Khasan?"

Paul looked down at his watch—ten thirty.

"I am hidden, so yes. Gennady came and was able to sneak me out of the republic during the night, bypassing a checkpoint on the roads and going through a river that was just shallow enough—we thought we would be dead at one point, when the engine turned off in the middle of the water. By some miracle, Gennady was able to start it again and get me out. But I know that they are looking for me, and if they find me *anywhere* in Russia, they will take me back, and I *will* be killed."

"And the Russian government doesn't provide any protection?"

"Many in the government, the police, would turn me over if they found me."

Paul was, by this point, writing furiously on the pad on the seat next to him.

"Khasan, I will help you in any way that I can, do you understand?"

"Yes, and thank you. I won't forget your kindness."

With that, Khasan put Gennady back on the phone.

"Do you think he may qualify to be a refugee?"

"My advice would be, don't take that chance," Paul stated, stopping his pen and looking out the windshield toward the immigration courthouse. "If he is rejected, and he very well may be, he will remain in danger."

"What do you suggest we do, then?"

"Get him *here*," Paul stated. "I believe he is a candidate for either asylum or as a Convention Against Torture case. What I would advise is to apply at the nearest U.S. consulate for a B-2 tourist visa."

"Yes," intoned Gennady. "I'm writing this down."

"He still owns his hair business at home, right? Make sure he tells them that at the consulate—they're going to want to know that he has continued ties in Russia, things that people in normal circumstances are not likely to walk away from."

"Yes, the salon is still in his name," Gennady confirmed.

"Does he have his passport?"

"Yes, of course."

"Wonderful," Paul replied. "Has he travelled outside of Russia recently?"

Gennady turned to ask Khasan that question. "France and Turkey—two and three years ago."

"*Perfect*—make sure they see that he has travelled as a tourist before."

"Okay," said Gennady, scribbling down the information as they talked.

"And be sure to tell them about his brother here in the States—that's why he's traveling, *right*? To see his brother. Visiting his brother provides a legal reason for him to request entry into the United States."

"Okay."

"I'm assuming you can get him to Moscow?"

"Yes."

"Once he has a visa, book a *direct flight* from Moscow to New York—no stops, do you understand? He has to fly directly, because if he has a layover in another European country, they will ask why he did not seek asylum there. After he arrives in the United States legally, he has one year to request asylum. I would not advise him to do that at the airport when first he arrives."

"And that is something you can help with—asylum?"

"Yes," Paul replied. "It is what is called affirmative asylum. We will have to show that he is in danger of being harmed if he goes home, either by the government or by a group the government can't control, and that he's at risk of being harmed anywhere in Russia because he's in a particular social group—in this case, being gay. Now, the hardest hurdle will be showing what's called 'visible sociability.' It can be difficult to argue that he's a visible minority—it has been very difficult to argue this in the past, but it's getting better."

"I understand."

"The other option is to present him as a Convention Against Torture case. We would need to show that it's more likely than not that he would be tortured or killed if returned to his country."

"Would photographs of injuries help?"

"You have *photos* of his injuries?"

"Of course, I am a photographer."

"Yes, that would be very helpful. He has no criminal record?"

"No."

"Excellent," Paul answered, glancing at his watch again—it was twenty-five minutes to eleven. "I have to go, but listen, fill out the form and get your appointment at the consulate."

"Yes, we will do this tonight," Gennady replied. "Can I call you at this same time next week?"

"Please do," Paul replied, collecting his things. "And please let Khasan know that when he lands in New York, I will be there with Anzor to pick him up."

"You realize you're saving a life, right?"

"I will do what I can to help."

"Would you be willing to help with other cases, if we had them?"

"How many cases are we talking about?" Paul asked, closing the door and clicking the key fob until the car chirped.

"We've got seventeen out of the republic and hiding now, and forty-four who have made contact."

Paul stopped in his tracks. "And these are all *similar* cases?"

"Men and women both, yes."

"I will do anything I can," Paul answered.

"God bless you, then, *Advokat.*"

"I'll talk with you next week."

Once he'd crossed the street and gone through the security checkpoint, he found his way to the men's room. After closing the stall door behind him, he fumbled with his phone while steadying himself with one hand on the wall, his body racked with sobs. He wiped his face with his palm and pulled himself together enough to make a call. Each ring in his ear seemed spaced apart as if there were whole minutes between them. He checked his watch one last time—ten fifty-two.

"Daniela? *Mi amor*—yes, I'm okay, I'm okay. Listen, I have to go into court right now, but can you please call Gabriel? Tell him to come this weekend. And … tell him we'd like to meet Benjamin, too."

**Fin.**

# CAST NO SHADOW

---

The wispy cirrus clouds of late spring floated listlessly, lavender and ethereal, in the endless expanse beyond the balmy orange glow of street lamps hung in neat rows throughout Nixon Estates Trailer Park. Venus and Jupiter luminously piercing the starless night, resplendent mementos to the vastness of the universe, like the depths of a lover's sparkling eyes, to anyone who might yield a moment to take them in. The ardent couple lay side by side, glistening and panting in the dark, three-speed electric fan oscillating on the dresser.

You think the neighbors heard me? she whispered.

The windows are open, Annabelle—wouldn't surprise me if the governor heard you all the way up in Austin.

She covered her flushed face with a pillow.

You sure are cute when you're embarrassed.

Shut up, Beau, came the muffled reply.

Besides, I ain't so worried about the neighbors as I am bout you wakin' up our son in the next room.

You think he hears us? she asked while sitting up quickly.

These walls are thick as a moth's wings. I think you're lucky he's a heavy sleeper.

Like his daddy.

And he snores like his mama.

I do not.

You ain't never heard yourself.

Of course, I ain't—cuz I don't snore.

You're cute when you argue, too.

Do you ever think I ain't cute?

When we're arguin' and I know you're right.

Well, I don't snore.

You're cute.

You're a good man, Beau Moreland, she said as she laid her head on his bare chest.

You're a good woman, yourself.

Their breathing morphed into synchrony as if they were one organism.

Cal's got baseball tomorrow afternoon, she stated quietly.

Game or practice?

Game.

What time?

Four.

I'll be there.

You workin' tomorrow night?

Gots to.

I sure hate when you work.

Why?

Cuz it's dangerous.

I'm good at what I do, woman.

I ain't said you wasn't.

Then why you worried?

It's still dangerous.

Ain't any more dangerous than being in Nam, and I did that four years.

She didn't say anything.

Plus, this ain't no big one. In and out like always.

Where?

You know I can't tell you that.

She frowned and squeezed him tight.

You're cute when you're worried, too.

Just don't get hurt, Beau.

Quitchyer fussin' and go to sleep before I get in the mood again.

Can I have the blanket?

Not if you're layin' on me.

I wanna lay on you, but I need the blanket, too.

Woman, it's eighty-four degrees.

I still need the blanket.

Then lay over there.

They fell asleep mingled and intertwined.

As the sun's first light breached the plastic blinds across the window, their limbs were still entangled, and the blanket was pulled up to her ears.

He got out of bed first, put his shorts on, and stumbled toward the bathroom.

Hi daddy.

Morning son, he answered as he pissed with his back toward the open door.

You comin' to my game this afternoon?

Sure am.

I'm line leader at school today.

Good for you.

Miss Dalton said I done such a good job last time that I could do it again.

I'm right proud of you.

He washed his face and put on his deodorant under Cal's watchful eye.

Only one more week and you're a fourth-grader.

Yeah.

You excited?

I'm more excited for summer break.

I was, too, when I was your age.

How long ago was that?

He chuckled and thought for a moment.

About twenty-five years, I reckon.

And how long ago since mama was nine years old?

About seventeen.

She younger'n you?

By a bit.

Y'all shouldn't be talkin' about a lady's age, it's bad manners, she said from the hall.

Boy can't know how old his own mama is?

It's just bad manners is all I'm sayin'.

Mornin', mama.

Mornin', my little man. You want cereal for breakfast?

We got Count Chocula?

Yeah. Some.

Okay.

The three sat at the table and ate.

What you doin' today, Beau?

Fixin' that fence for Mrs. Watson.

What's wrong with it?

Old Deputy Royce drove clear through it Sunday night, drunker'n'hell.

That's gonna take you all day?

You ain't seen the fence.

Okay. But four o'clock, right?

Yeah, I'll be there. You workin' today?

I got late shift.

When you home?

Nine.

Okay, that'll work.

Beau walked his son down the dusty lane to the front gate of the park where the bus would pick him up for school.

What three things I always want you to remember, son?

You'll always love me—

—No matter what.

A real man helps those who can't help themselves.

And number three?

Don't take no shit from nobody.

Good.

The bus pulled up with a belch of smoke and stopped to gather the thirty or so children of the park.

Have a good day.

I love you, daddy.

I love you, too, son.

Beau watched his boy climb the steps and find his seat toward the back. The two waved at each other as the bus lurched forward and drove off.

He spent the day fixing Mrs. Watson's fence and was home in time to shower before leaving to watch Cal play ball. The boy went two for four with an RBI.

When it was over, Beau rustled his son's hair.

You wanna take the bus or ride with me?

Ride with you.

Okay.

They ate spam and grilled cheese and sliced tomatoes for dinner. Beau bathed the boy and dressed him in his dinosaur pajamas before laying with him and letting him labor through his reading homework.

You workin' tonight, daddy?

Yeah.

The boy was silent.

Why you ask?

Just wanted to know.

Okay.

Will you give me a kiss when you come in?

I always do.

I know.

You do?

Yeah.

So, what, you're just pretendin' to sleep?

No, I'm sleepin', but I still feel you kiss me. And I like to know you got home safe—I sleep better.

Why's everyone so worried about me?

Mama says you have a dangerous job.

Not more dangerous than most, if you know how to do it right.

And you know how to do it right?

Me and the boys, yeah.

Okay.

You don't need to worry you none, boy.

I won't.

Good.

But you'll still come in and kiss me?

Of course.

With a hug and a kiss on the top of the head, Beau headed out into the hall, closing the door gently behind him. He popped a cold can of Lone Star and shuffled through a folder of maps until he found one for the greater Laredo area and spread it across the wicker coffee table. He sat on the edge of the sofa and studied it while he drank his beer.

At quarter after nine Annabelle came in.

Hey, baby.

How was work?

Slow.

She tossed her apron on the kitchen counter and collapsed next to him on the sofa.

I have a sip?

He handed her his beer and she took a manly swig.

You okay?

Just tired, she answered as she passed the can back to him. Only made twenty-two dollars in tips on a ten-hour shift.

You know you ain't got to work, right?

Why wouldn't I work, Beau?

Cuz you ain't got to.

But I want to.

Okay. You wanna give me a blowjob, too?

Not if I ain't got to, she chuckled.

You ain't got to, he smiled.

Cal's game good?

Yeah, he done good.

Good. I'm a take a shower and lay down.

Okay. I'm fixin' to leave. Rendezvous is at ten-thirty.

He smacked her ass as she got up from the sofa.

Ouch!

That's for drinkin' my beer.

She flipped him the bird over her shoulder on her way down the hall.

What a good woman, he thought.

He folded up the map and swigged the last from the can. In the bedroom he pulled a black duffle bag out from under the bed and zipped it open. He double checked its contents and then zipped it closed. From the closet he donned a black hunting shirt and his black army boots. He double checked his Model 92 Beretta from the top shelf and holstered it under his shirt.

The water went off and after a minute or two Annabelle entered the bedroom, hair wrapped in one towel, her slender frame wrapped in another.

I'm outta here, gorgeous.

Be careful, Beau.

Always am.

I love you.

Love you, too.

They kissed and embraced.

A moment later he tossed the black bag on the passenger seat of his pickup and cranked the engine. Down the row of trailers, under the orange lights, a few teenagers straddled their bikes and drank cheap beers. They nodded to him as he waved to them.

In twenty minutes, he was parked behind Clyde's bar, two spaces from the dumpster. Within five more, the brothers Avery and Sterling Merrick pulled in on his right. At ten twenty-one, Bronco parked to the right of them. Ninety seconds later, Miles Hickson parked to his left. At ten-thirty on the dot, Lynn Marshall pulled in. All soldiers were accounted for. They piled into two trucks and headed down 83 toward a ranch they'd staked out on the western outskirts of Laredo. They were mostly silent, aside from a couple reminders about operational specifics.

In about an hour and forty minutes' time, they pulled off on a dirt road and a couple miles down before shutting off their headlights. They parked on the east side of the ridge and geared up.

Twenty minutes? asked Sterling.

Twenty-five, answered Lynn, after glancing down into the well-lit valley.

Okay.

The brothers stayed behind while the band of four pulled black masks over their faces and then disappeared into the darkness round

the bend. Sterling unpacked his sniper rifle while Avery began sur-
veilling the scene below with binoculars.

What you see?

Two guards.

How far apart?

Hundred-sixty meters.

Anything on the north side?

Nothing.

Good.

They made their calculations and bided their time.

Been twenty-five yet?

Thirty seconds more.

I'm gonna give them another minute—at least until this sonofabitch crosses back in front of the truck.

Avery nodded silently.

The compound guard wore cowboy boots and hat, blue jeans,
and a white shirt, an M16 slung round his shoulders. When Sterling
pulled the trigger, the heavy caliber round blew the heart clear out
of his chest. He spun and collapsed, face first into the pickup and
then into the dirt. His myocardium continued to throb on the earth
beside him.

For dust thou art and unto dust shalt thou return.

Amen, answered Avery.

The brothers fixed their attention on the second guard, who was
completely unaware of the fate that had befallen his compatriot. He
was similarly unaware of the fate that befell him, as he departed this
world before what would remain of him hit the ground.

Sterling and Avery kept watch to maintain a secure perimeter
around the compound as their fellow soldiers prepared to enter the
main building.

Bronco kicked the door in and entered guns blazing. The door-
man, a large man with correspondingly large beard, was blown out

of his chair before he could reach for his weapon. Two more were dispatched in similar fashion. Commotion and shouting ensued as the squad pushed their way into the main room of the warehouse.

Hands up, motherfuckers! Lynn shouted.

Rows and rows of women, mostly Mexican, lifted their hands at their seats. Possibly thirty tables were lined, end to end, in three neat rows, who knew how much heroin being weighed, measured, and packaged on each.

Beau caught a flash of motion from the corner of his eye and downed a biker as he darted into the room.

Where's T-rex? Beau demanded.

The women simply stared.

What am I talkin' Chinese? Where the fuck is T-rex?

One elderly woman pointed toward a door in the rear of the large room.

Lynn, you stay put?

Lynn nodded.

Don't any of you move a fucking inch, you hear?

Beau, Bronco, and Miles made their way through the rows of tables and opened the back door. The hallway was long and looked like it actually connected two different buildings. They started down it stealthily and cautiously. When they reached the door at the far end, Beau tried the handle and opened it quietly. Two men, clad in leather and indicative patches, were reclined on sofas, watching the tv in the corner of the office.

Show me your hands, motherfuckers, and don't think about moving, Beau said quietly. We ain't the po-lice either and we don't mind cappin' your asses.

Miles and Bronco rushed in and put the bikers on the ground, zip-tying their hands behind their backs.

Where's T-rex? Miles asked, barrel of his gun in the back of one captive's neck.

Bathroom, he answered.

Where?

He nodded his head toward the corner of the room.

Bronco, do us the honor?

With that, the enormous man kicked the bathroom door in. T-rex stood quickly, handful of toilet paper and pants around his ankles. The look on his face was priceless.

Oh goddamn, Beau shouted. Wipe your ass and come out here, nasty motherfucker.

T-rex complied and in a minute he was tied to his office chair, Beau seated on his desk.

Nice little operation you got going here. Too bad you didn't think decent security was worth the investment, huh?

You want the dope?

Fuck no. That shit ain't nothin' but poison.

That poison's worth a lot of fucking money.

I don't want no dope.

Then what you want?

The money you're holding, you dumb sonofabitch.

It ain't here.

T-rex, T-rex—don't insult my intelligence.

It ain't here, man.

With that, Beau blew a hole in his knee.

Oh, fuck, man! Oh, holy fuck!

T-rex spun in his office chair with his good foot.

Where's the *money*, T-rex?

It ain't fuckin' here!

I'm gonna let what just happened to you sink in for ten seconds, and then you're either gonna tell me where the money is, or you're gonna lose your other kneecap, too.

Man, it ain't here!

Ten.

I can't tell you—

Nine.

It's in a safe in the walk-in freezer!

Wow. Now was that worth the pain you're dealing with right now?

Fuck you, man, came the terse reply from T-rex, saliva running down his chin.

Sit tight, T-rex, Beau said with a smile.

Bronco stood one of the captives up off the floor and inspected his name patch.

Okay, Groucho, show us the freezer.

Beau gave the signal and Bronco and Miles departed with the zip-tied Groucho.

I know who you are, T-rex said through a contorted smile.

Shut the fuck up.

I know who you are, motherfucker.

You ain't got the first clue.

It don't matter. You fucked with the wrong ranch tonight—

Shut the fuck up.

You shoulda done your homework.

You don't think I did my homework?

T-rex grimaced and laughed simultaneously.

How you think I knew how to get in here? How you think I knew you were sittin' on a shit-ton of cash? How you think I knew security was so lax?

Don't matter.

And why not?

Cuz it's not *if* security's lax, it's *why*.

You're a comedian, ain't you?

And you're the dumbest motherfucker I ever seen.

You're about to lose your other kneecap.

Security ain't tight because nobody with two braincells to rub together would fuck with this place.

Why—cuz they gonna have to listen to you talk?

Cuz this ain't a gang ranch, that's why.

You're a piece of work, you know that?

This ain't no biker ranch. You just fucked with a straight up cartel ranch, you dumb shit.

Those words froze the pulse blue in Beau's veins.

You fucked now, T-rex said with a grim laugh.

With that, his other kneecap shattered and the chair tipped forward, planting T-rex face down on the floor and in agony.

When Miles and Bronco came back with Groucho, they told Beau the money was ready to haul.

They signaled Avery and Sterling on the hill to pull the trucks down and they got to packing. Lynn and Miles led the women and the remaining—living—bikers outside, dragging a shrieking T-rex along the ground by his shoulders. Once the trucks were loaded, the building and its contents were set ablaze, and the soldiers were off in the dark.

After fifteen minutes of precautionary elusive maneuvers, the gang were back on the road to Clyde's in silence. Back at the bar, they entered through a private door behind the dumpster and began the process of spilling cash into counting machines. An hour later they had one point four million separated into six even stacks, less fifty thousand owed to Clyde for his services and rent.

There were eight safes in the room—seven of them rather large. Each member put ten thousand into one single safe—the *equipment and expenses*, or *retained earnings*, safe, as Bronco liked to joke. Varying amounts were put in each individual's safe. Miles deposited Clyde's earnings in the single small safe, knowing it would be cleared out by the owner before daylight.

They went out and sat at the bar for a few beers together, played a couple rounds of pool, and then capped off the evening with shots of tequila.

Nice work tonight, boys, Beau said, raising his glass.

Same to you, Cap.

Y'all do some good with your paychecks, you hear?

Yes, sir.

They shook hands and parted in separate directions—Avery and Sterling out the front door, Bronco out the back, and Lynn to the hooker on the far end of the bar.

A word, soldier? Beau asked Miles.

Sure thing, boss.

In the back room with the counting machines and safes, Beau paced for a moment and then sat on the edge of a table.

What is it, boss?

Whose ranch was that we hit tonight?

Road Hawks, why?

How sure are you?

How sure am I of what?

That it was Road Hawks we hit.

You saw T-rex there, didn't you?

Yeah, I saw him there, but I'm wondering how sure you are that we hit a biker ranch.

Why?

I'm asking you, Miles.

I'm positive.

One hundred percent?

One hundred percent.

Okay.

Why you asking? You ain't never asked me before.

That's cuz you're good at your job, Miles.

What's changed now?

A little something T-rex said to me.

What'd that little bitch say?

I don't mean to alarm you, but he said it was a cartel ranch.

What?

A cartel ranch.

No fucking way—that little shit was fucking with your mind.

Beau gave him a stern look.

There's no way, boss! I checked it—I swear to God.

I trust you, Miles. But is there *any* chance—any small, slight chance at all—that you reckon we need to tell the others—just out of precaution?

No way. I did my recon, boss—I did my job.

Okay. You know I trust you with my life.

I don't take that lightly—never have.

I know, soldier.

The two men stood in silence for a long moment.

That dumb little bitch was just running his mouth, boss. They say an empty wagon makes the most noise.

Beau managed a subdued chuckle, and with that, he patted Miles on the shoulder and walked over toward his safe. He pulled small canvas bags out of the cabinet on the wall and filled them each with one hundred thousand dollars. He put twenty thousand in his black duffle bag and slung it over his shoulder.

You make sure you treat Annabelle and Cal to some of that, too, boss.

Oh, we're alright. There's a lotta people needing help more'n us.

Your family deserves a nice life, too, Cap.

Beau looked at him while a coy smile curled on his upper lip.

We *got* a nice life.

Miles nodded silently.

You be careful out there, soldier.

You, too, boss.

When Beau got home, the first thing he did was put his bags of money in the safe buried face up under the house. Then he put his duffle bag away in the closet with great stealth. He was so anxious to climb into Annabelle's arms that he almost forgot his promise to Cal. He opened the bedroom door slowly, wincing with every creak. He approached the boy's bed and sat down gingerly on the edge. The street light pierced the corner of the blind and threw an orange glow across the boy's freckled face. Beau sat silently for a moment, watching his child breathe. He leaned in and kissed that soft, angelic face, and had to hold back the sudden well of emotion that nearly choked him. He took a piss, showered, and brushed his teeth before crawling into the bed beside his woman. He pulled the covers back and pressed himself against her warm body.

Not tonight, baby.

Why not?

Cuz I'm sleeping.

No, you ain't.

I was.

You ain't now.

I gotta be up in an hour, baby. You can hold me, though.

It's too hot for all that.

Okay.

He chuckled to himself and rolled over. She pulled the covers back up over her shoulders.

I'm glad you're home safe, though.

Me, too, he said, kicking a leg out from under the blanket.

The last thing that crossed his mind before he slept was the delicate smell of her and how much she felt like home—the home he'd never had.

She was gone for the morning shift before he awoke and had already fed Cal a pop-tart.

Beau walked his son though the trailer park and down to the street to meet the bus.

You got a game today?

Just practice.

Beau nodded.

The two stood quietly, the father sipping his coffee.

Three things, right?

Yes, sir.

What are they?

You'll always love me no matter what.

Number two?

Real men help those who can't help themselves.

Right. And last?

Don't take no shit—

—No shit from nobody.

The man tussled his boy's hair.

Thanks for kissing me last night, daddy.

You were awake?

No.

Then how'd you know I done it?

I just know'd it.

The man smiled as the bus pulled up.

I love you, buddy.

Love you, too, daddy.

Have a good day, he called as the boy climbed the steps into the bus. Cal waved his arm without turning back.

The backside of their trailer faced the backside of the park, with just trees and shrubs at the end of their yard. Beau had put up some lattice privacy fences as well, to keep peering eyes out of his backyard. Initially, the thought had been to prevent the teenagers next door from ogling his pretty little wife when she laid out to tan, but the fences also served to shield view from his comings and goings under the house. He sat in silence at the picnic table with a cup of coffee and listened. Everyone was gone to work or school. He climbed under the trailer and pulled two of three duffels out. He put them on the floorboard of the passenger's side of the truck.

Down the road about ten miles, he came into the center of town and headed north through the square. He parked outside Morse Bank and Trust and met Lyle Morse, bank manager and son of founder Jedediah Morse, in his office. The two men shook hands firmly and sat opposing each other at Lyle's desk.

Same as usual, Mr. Moreland?

I'd like to do something a little different today, Mr. Morse.

Shoot.

Fifty grand to the children's hospital, like always—

Okay, the banker replied while writing in a notebook.

Fifty grand to the old folks' home—

As usual.

And I wanna make sure that's going to pay for folks who can't afford it.

Naturally.

Ten thousand to the Morse Family Trust.

Thank you, again, sir.

Ten to the drug rehab center in Lakehurst. Ten to the rehab center in Woodside.

Okay—

Ten to the VFW. Ten to the food pantry.

Of course—and just to be clear, we're still anonymous on all these?

Just like always.

Okay.

Lyle Morse stared down at his pad and then looked up.

And the remaining fifty?

Beau was silent for a moment.

I wanna set up a trust or something.

A trust?

Something to take care of Cal in case—

The banker nodded slowly.

In case something was to happen to me.

Sure. We can help you with that. We may need the services of an attorney, depending on how you'd like to proceed. Starting with fifty thousand?

I'll have another fifty for you next week.

Okay, so let's start there.

I need it clean, too—*washed*, if you know what I mean.

Mr. Moreland, you've anonymously contributed nearly half a million dollars to my family's trust, and we've been doing business for a long time. I can assure you that it will be taken care of on my end.

Thank you.

Yes, sir.

When Beau walked out the front door of the bank, his two canvas bags were empty. He walked around his truck slowly, checked all four tires, then popped the hood. He glanced over the engine, making sure everything was in its proper place.

A single engine Cessna rumbled in low over the town on its final approach to the airstrip off highway fifteen. Beau stopped and got a tuna sandwich at the local family-run diner, then headed home to sleep some more. He woke after two, brushed his teeth and dressed in time to watch Cal's practice at the ball field. The man and boy stopped to pick up a Hot n' Ready on the way home.

There was the usual gaggle of teenagers of all shapes, sizes, and colors on bikes and skateboards nearly blocking the entrance to Nixon's. Beau slowed down and cursed them under his breath as he pulled in. He forced a smile and a wave as they languidly parted down the middle to allow his truck to pass. Out of his periphery he caught a gaze that was out of place. Seated on a picnic table to his left was a Mexican whose cold stare followed the truck as it proceeded through the throng of unoccupied youngsters. The young man locked eyes with Beau, who slowly tipped his hat. The teen did nothing. Beau felt a shiver rush up his spine as he clenched his teeth. The truck pulled down Sycamore Terrace. A quick glance in the rearview gave him some measure of relief, as the teen's attention had relocated upon a tall blonde in tiny shorts.

Why you goin' this way, Daddy?

Just wanna check on someone real quick.

But I'm hungry.

Ain't gonna take more than a minute, son.

The boy sighed and tightened his grip around the pizza box.

Beau continued to monitor his mirrors. A bulldog and a rat terrier strolled side by side down the lane. Old Mrs. Eckert watered her tulips and bluebonnets in her flower print housedress. A toddler rode her three-wheeler confidently through her yard and her neighbor's. The truck wove through the grid of streets—the man distractedly aware of his surroundings, the boy aware only of the rumbling of his stomach and the aroma of heaven emanating from the hot carton in his lap.

Once he was as satisfied as he'd ever be, Beau pulled down his street and parked in his driveway. Cal jumped out of the truck and ran straight into the house with dinner, leaving his backpack and all in the floorboard. His father got out much more slowly, taking a deliberate and three-sixty-degree survey of the scene. Nothing out of place.

Inside the doublewide, Cal was halfway through his second slice, while Annabelle was washing dishes in a pair of cutoff shorts that immediately drew the man's gaze to her firm, supple legs.

Hey, baby, she called.

Hey.

Something wrong?

No.

You sure?

Yeah.

Okay. You wanna slice before Cal eats it all?

Uh, yeah.

Here's a clean plate.

Thank you.

She quickly towel-dried a thin white plate and leaned in to hand it to him while simultaneously standing on one tiptoe to kiss him on the cheek.

You look like you done seen a ghost, she said, stepping backward toward the sink.

It's nothin, baby—just got a lot on my mind.

Well, she stared back toward him with a teasing glance. She put her arms around him and stood on her tiptoes again to whisper in his ear. Maybe after junior is asleep, I can help clear your mind.

Sounds good, baby.

Her gut told her something still wasn't right. He opened the fridge and cracked open a beer without asking her if she wanted anything like he normally did. She watched him steal glances out the window by the table as he ate. In those shorts, his eyes would normally be glued on her.

As night fell, she thought he seemed increasingly on edge. He practically paced from room to room, peering out windows and checking and rechecking locks on the doors. She sat on the sofa, legs curled under her, watching tv, but mostly watching him. Finally, he plopped down next to her and let out a sigh.

Baby, do we need to talk about something?

No, why?

Cuz you're acting like you're expecting someone—someone uninvited.

Don't be silly.

Beau, she furrowed her brow and turned his face toward hers.

Don't worry, Annabelle. Why you gotta worry all the time?

I don't worry all the time, but I'm worrying a little bit now.

Why just now?

Cuz you're acting weird.

Am not.

Don't you lie to me, Beau Moreland.

He chewed his lip and then swigged his beer.

There was a new kid in the neighborhood when I pulled in tonight.

So?

He didn't look like he belonged.

Kids are in and out of here all the time—you know that.

Yeah, but with him there was something … *off*.

Off?

It was almost like he was looking for me—*waiting* for me.

Did he say anything to you?

No, he just stared.

He just stared?

Yeah.

And that's it?

He nodded.

And that's what's got my man—my tough, soldier-man—all worked up?

He shrugged.

Well, if that's all it is, I think I help you relax a little better.

He half-smiled.

She got up and took his hand, and the two went back to the bedroom.

When it was over, and she was asleep on his chest, he stared up at the ceiling, a tightness in his throat. He sat up slowly and repositioned her head on a pillow, then rolled over and gazed out the window. A few moments later he checked the doors again. He took a leak and then went into Cal's room. The boy was laying sideways, across his bed. Beau gently picked up his son and turned him back longways. He kissed his forehead and then went back to bed himself.

A coyote baying off in the distance. Tree frogs. Silence.

He laid his head back and took a few deep breaths. After sitting up and glancing once more at his handgun on the night table, his fingers delicately running down the barrel to the stock, he closed his eyes slowly and allowed himself to drift.

Somewhere between his restless countenance and his buried ego, he dreamed of jungles and rivers, snakes and saolas. Heat and stifling humidity, maggots and mice, he was oddly at peace in this middle ground between vigilance and torpidity. He was only awakened, and slowly at that, by a slow scratching sound. He sat up silently and listened. No howling coyotes. No screeching frogs. Just nebulous scratching.

Pistol in hand, he followed the sound out into the hall, popping his head into his son's bedroom quickly to see him soundly sleeping. Beau followed his ears into the living room and lowered his weapon toward the front door. The sound came in rhythmic threesomes. In the dark, a sparkle of orange gleamed on the doorknob as it seemed to start to turn. Suddenly a creak from the hall made him spin on his heels and aim.

Daddy?

Beau dropped his hands and choked back a cough.

Cal, what are you doing up?

I need a drink.

Beau looked back down at the front door handle.

Everything okay?

Yeah, yeah, buddy. Can you go back to bed?

Will you get me some water?

Yeah, just a second.

The boy shuffled back down the hall and into his room.

Beau unbolted the lock and swung the door open, pistol drawn. He heard an engine rev down the street and nearly leapt outside to get a make on it. A small motorcycle sped through the stop sign at an intersection and was gone. He checked the immediate area and found nothing amiss. He went back inside and locked the door behind him. He poured a glass of water and took it to Cal only to find the boy dormant again. He carried the boy into the other bedroom and placed him down next to his mother. He got his shotgun off the top shelf of the closet and plopped down on the sofa with it in his lap. He sat there in silence until the sun came up.

Hey, baby, Annabelle said as she wiped her eyes.

Hey.

Cal kick you outta bed? He hasn't done that since he was tiny.

No, I put him in there.

Why you got the *shotgun* out?

I thought ... I thought somebody tried to get in here last night.

*What?*

It might have been nothin—just didn't want to take any chances.

He finally lifted his glance from the inside of the door to his wife. He wasn't prepared for the anger on her face.

Beau Moreland. You promised me you would never bring that shit home.

I didn't, Annabelle.

Seems like you *did*. You weren't acting right when you got home and then you spent the night on the sofa with a shotgun in your lap.

Annabelle—

Listen to me, Beau, the only reason I signed up for this was because you promised me—

It ain't come home.

If her glare was steel, it would have bored a hole straight through him.

You *cannot*, Beau. Your *son* is in there.

I know that, woman.

Then you have to tell me, what is going on?

It ain't nothin you gotta worry about—

—But it is *something*, and not just some teenager that looked at you funny.

I don't know for sure.

Police?

He looked back at the door.

It ain't the police, is it?

I don't think it's anything, Annabelle. It was just some stupid shit somebody said. I'd been thinking about that and then I saw that new kid out there yesterday and I just didn't sleep well. That's really all there is to it.

I have a hard time believing that's all there is to it.

You don't trust me, woman?

Of course, I *trust* you, but you know I've never asked you to do this.

The work I do makes a difference in the world.

So does working in the plant, Beau. So does rigging oil.

Those are jobs, and you're fooling yourself if you think they ain't dangerous, too.

Her head and her shoulders heaved slowly.

But they ain't *war*.

War is all I know.

On our own soil? In our own neighborhood?

A tight lump rose in his chest.

I didn't ask for it, Annabelle. You've seen what that white shit's done to this country. We don't have to look any further than our

129

own kin. And if those fucking Mexicans weren't bringing it over the border in—

That's a lie, Beau. You know it is.

His tongue crept over his bottom lip.

They wouldn't be bringing it over the border if we didn't want it. They're making a living for their family just like you. Plus, we got our own gangs making their own shit right here.

It's against the law and it's against human dignity, he retorted.

And killing ain't?

Not if what you're killing ain't human.

Beau—

Her flush face found itself buried in her hands. Welling eyes peered at him through gaps in slender fingers.

Have you ever considered that maybe it makes you less human?

Is that what you think of me—that I've become some sort of a monster?

Of course, I don't, Beau—I'm not trying to make you upset—

Am I not a loving husband? A loving father?

You're the best man I could have ever dreamed of—

Then what are you trying to say?

It's got to change a man—it's *got* to. How can you do what you do and not have something change on the inside?

You wanna know what changed me? Watching my best friend bleed out in a jungle from a gunshot that severed the artery in his neck. Seeing men I worked with—lived with, depended on—get blown to kingdom fuck by explosives tied to a little kid who went up and gave 'em a hug. Finding my own brother in a pool of his own vomit—

She put her hand on the back of his neck and drew him toward her.

At least I'm fighting *for* something this time, Annabelle. Doesn't that make a difference?

Of course, it does, baby.

He pressed his face into her stomach.

You're a good man, Beau. I've never doubted that for a second—I want you to know that.

Looking up at her, he asked, I can stop at least some of it, can't I?

Yeah, you might—but it still ain't gonna bring Mason back.

She knelt in front of him and drew his face toward hers for a kiss.

You don't have to keep doing this.

I wouldn't know what else to do.

You could figure that out.

He shrugged and managed a half smile.

I'm gonna be late for work, she said.

Okay.

You should go back in and try to sleep. I'll leave some breakfast out for Cal. He can just watch cartoons when he gets up.

It's Saturday, that's right.

I'll be home after four, okay?

Sounds good.

Maybe we could go to Ponderosa and then go see a movie or something tonight?

That'd be nice.

It's been a while since we've done something as a family.

Yeah, it has.

She turned and went back down the hall to shower and dress for work.

After she'd left, he got back in bed next to his son. He put his arms around him and drifted off.

The phone startled him, and he quickly reach for his handgun and his watch at once. It was after noon. The bed was empty next to him.

Cal?

Yeah? the answer came from down the hall.

Get the phone?

Okay.

Muffled talking from the next room.

Then, the boy appeared at the door.

It's Mr. Miles for you.

Miles?

Yeah. He sounds worried.

Beau popped out of bed and raced past the boy and down the hall.

Miles, he said as he put the handset to his ear.

You hear about Bronco?

No, what about him?

He was in an accident last night, Cap.

An *accident*?

He was on 85 headed out of Carrizo Springs and his truck run off the road. Hit a telephone pole head on.

Is he okay?

He's in the hospital and they're not sure he's gonna make it.

Fuck.

Cal watched from the hall near the kitchenette.

Was Tina with him?

No, he was alone.

Is someone with her now?

Her sister.

Good.

And, boss—there's something else.

What?

I came through that way this morning and … there's tire tread all over the place.

Tell me what that means, Miles.

I think there was another car involved.

Somebody hit him?

No, but close. I think somebody might have ran him off the road.

Beau's eyes met his son's.

Boss?

Yeah, I'm here.

Look, I don't think it's anything to worry about. I know he was drinking and he might have just got hot with somebody out there or something. You know what his temper's like when he drinks.

Yeah.

You think we should be worried?

He turned away from his son.

I think we should be *cautious*, he said quietly.

I'll keep you posted.

Okay.

He hung the phone in its cradle slowly.

Everything okay, Daddy?

Yes, son. One of my friends was in a bad accident last night.

Is he okay?

I'm not sure.

I'm sorry.

Beau smiled at his son.

You hungry?

I fixed a sandwich.

Well, look at you.

The boy shrugged.

Tell you what, let me make a cup of coffee and then we'll go down to the field and play catch—how's that sound?

The edges of the boy's smile nearly touched both his ears.

The only white in the sky that day was a spinning, hurtled base-ball. Two sounds pierced the humid atmosphere: the snap of cow-hide around cowhide and laughter. Man and boy at play.

Beau didn't even notice the crowd of teenagers that had amassed near the dugout until Cal threw one over his head. As he turned to chase the ball he saw them—many of the same kids from Nixon Estates. He scanned the herd while retrieving the ball. No sign of the out of place Mexican from the previous day. One youngster, whose name he thought for some reason might be Todd, smiled at him and nodded his head. Beau nodded back politely. He checked his watch as he turned back toward Cal.

It's after four, he said. Whataya say we head back to the house?

Can't we play a few more minutes? the sweaty boy pleaded.

Nah, I think we should get back and clean up—your mama will be home soon and we're all going out tonight.

We are?

Yeah.

To do what?

Ponderosa and a movie.

Yes!

The boy nearly sprinted toward the truck.

Beau chuckled and tossed the ball in the air. He caught it overhead and then began jogging toward the truck himself. Anamorphic memories of his high school playing days teased his attention until he saw the Mexican teen sitting on the hood of a Trans Am parked next to his truck.

Cal, hold up.

The boy kept running, nearly there.

Cal, wait!

The Mexican's stare turned from the man and followed the boy past him and into the truck. Only then did his gaze turn back to Beau.

What the fuck do you want?

The silent aloofness sent a cold shudder through Beau's body.

Before he knew it, he had the kid by the shirt and pinned him to the ground.

What are you staring at?

The teen flashed a golden smile that was as false as it was carefree.

Incoherent shouting pierced the din over Beau's shoulder as the gaggle of juveniles hurriedly approached. With two fistfuls of t-shirt he was shoving the Mexican into the dirt over and over until he felt a strong hand on his shoulder.

Mr. Moreland!

Beau spun back and shoved Todd backward with enough force to cause him to stagger and fall. There were perhaps six others standing there in a mixture of apprehension and concern. Beau's surroundings came into focus, and he realized he was breathing heavily. He looked down at the Mexican beneath him and was met by that same indifferent smile.

Mr. Moreland, Todd said, climbing back to his feet. That's my cousin, sir.

Beau stood up quickly and dusted his hands off nervously.

I'm sorry, he stammered.

The olive-skinned teen cocked himself up on one elbow and clicked his tongue over his top teeth.

He graduated last week and is down from El Paso visiting.

I'm sorry, Todd—I don't know what—

My name's *James*, sir.

I'm sorry, James.

You, okay, Julio? James asked.

He nodded slowly, eyes still locked on Beau.

The man extended his hand, but the kid pushed himself up and past Beau, their shoulders jostling as he went.

Come on, get in the truck, Beau commanded his son.

Cal was frozen in place, his eyes fixed on the Mexican.

I said, get in the truck.

The boy snapped to and opened the passenger door. As the truck backed up out of the parking spot, he kept his eyes fixed on the teen his father had assaulted. There surely was something not right about him. A cold shiver ran down the boy's spine as they drove away.

Sorry you had to see that, son.

You were sticking up for yourself.

I don't know if you could call it that.

You didn't take shit from that boy.

That's not ... Beau shook his head back and forth.

They drove in silence for a few moments.

Look, Beau started as they pulled into the main entrance of the trailer park. I lost myself a little bit back there. I shouldn't have done what I did.

The boy sat in silence.

What happened this afternoon was a mistake. That's all it was, plain and simple.

But that boy ain't dangerous?

No, at least ... No, I don't think so.

He looks dangerous to *me*.

Well, looking dangerous is one thing, son. *Being* dangerous is something completely different.

Annabelle was already home when they pulled in the driveway.

Listen, Beau said. You don't have to tell your mama about what happened, okay?

Okay, I won't.

It's a good thing to know that your daddy makes mistakes just like anybody else.

The boy nodded.

When I was your age, I didn't think my daddy could do any wrong.

What do you think about your daddy now?

Beau laughed.

I think he was a man, just like me.

The two sat in the truck for a minute, before Annabelle waved to them from the kitchen window.

Let's go in and get ready to eat.

Okay.

Beau put on his best airs when he got inside.

Why you all dusty? she asked almost immediately.

Oh, you know, we played hard out there.

Her nose was straight and thin, her brow was intelligent and soft, her lips rosy and thick. Her eyes were bright green with hazel specks dispersed at random. She stood there in her waitress uniform, playful half smile cocked on her face, and he thought she'd never looked more ravishing.

Boys will be boys, their son chimed in after a minute.

That's right, she answered. And apparently, they will always look like they came right in out of the barn.

Cal shrugged.

Go clean up, okay?

Okay.

After the boy went down the hall his father embraced his woman and kissed her deeply. She opened her eyes in surprise when their lips finally parted.

A little nap did you some good, huh?

He smiled and moved a strand of hair out of her face.

I think I want to retire.

You do?

I think so.

You know what I want, Beau.

I do.

But if you get out, I want you to get out because you decided to.

I am deciding.

She kissed him again.

You know that makes me happy, she said softly, laying her head on his shoulder.

I do.

Should we go celebrate?

Yeah, we should.

She went to change her clothes and he went to the phone. He called Miles but got no answer. He thought about trying the hospital to check on Bronco but decided against it. Nothing he would do could alter the situation—so he would enjoy the evening with his family and try Miles again that night.

The three ate and laughed and felt like a real family that evening. They went to a PG-13 action movie that Cal had been dying to see—one about heroes and villains in a world where it was unmistakable which was which. She held Beau's hand throughout most of the film and he spent ninety minutes basking in the luster of her.

On the drive home they laughed and sang, and their silly song was only interrupted by the presence of Lynn Marshall's truck in the gravel driveway.

What the fuck? Beau asked aloud.

As he cut the engine off, Lynn stepped out to greet them. His face was ashen, and he gritted his front teeth together and spat through them.

Hey Mr. Lynn! the boy called.

Hey young'un.

What are you doing here?

There's been—

Lynn made a guttural sound like he'd swallowed a frog.

What, Lynn?

It's Miles, man.

What about him?

He's *dead*.

Oh, my God, Annabelle gasped.

Beau's arms hung motionless as if they were lead pipes.

Go on, you two get inside, he finally stuttered.

Lynn gave a half smile in a joint effort to reassure the woman, and to conceal his own emotions—because that's what a man was supposed to do. When she and Cal were in the house, he turned back toward Beau, who was still standing like a piece of marble.

What the fuck happened, man? I just talked to him this afternoon.

I got a call from John Moss, the sheriff's deputy I go way back with, and he said they're calling it a murder-suicide.

What?

He killed Darla and then shot himself in the head, is what they're saying.

He killed Darla?

That's what they're saying.

Now Lynn, look at me—

They're eyes locked.

That just don't make no goddamn sense.

And I got some more bad news, Cap.

What now?

I talked to Tina's sister, and it don't look like Bronco's gonna make it.

Beau heaved as he struggled to keep his breath, then caught the glance of his son from the kitchen window. He waved and smiled at the boy's sullen glare.

How is Tina holding up?

As good as can be, I reckon.

I need a smoke.

The two men leaned against Beau's truck and lit cigarettes silently. The haze wafted from their lungs toward the great glow of the amber street lamp overhead.

You get in touch with Avery and Sterling?

Tried, but no luck, Lynn answered.

Goddamn.

What do we do, boss?

I think we head up to the cabin.

Lynn nodded.

You want me to stop by Clyde's?

No need. We all got enough to live on up there for a week or two, especially without …

I'll go home and get Chrissy and the kids packed up.

Okay. And on second thought, run by Clyde's and check in on the man, would you?

You want anything from the safe?

Nah—just make sure he knows what's up. He and his are welcome to hide out with us.

Sure thing, boss.

How long'll that take you?

Get up there and back home? We can meet you at the rendezvous point in, say, four hours?

Beau checked his watch.

Four hours.

Four hours.

And you be careful, soldier.

You, too, boss.

Beau watched Lynn's tail lights disappear around the corner as he lit another cigarette. He ran through a mental checklist of items they'd stored at the cabin in the hills, and items they'd need if they were going to lay low and out of sight for the time being. He chuckled to himself as he thought about having given up the game just that evening. It seemed the game was still playing him.

He opened the trailer door to see Annabelle sitting on the sofa, back rigid and hands on her knees.

What the hell's going on, Beau?

We need to head up to the cabin for a bit.

The cabin?

Yeah.

Goddamn, Beau—it's that serious?

I don't think so, but I don't wanna take no risks with my family either.

Her eyes closed, and her brow knotted.

I wish you'd thought of that beforehand—

We already been through this, woman. We ain't got no choice now. We hideout for a week or so and form a plan. We'll get out of here.

Out of where?

She opened her eyes and glared at him.

Out of Texas, maybe out of the country.

That's what *gettin' out* means to you—running away?

If we ain't got a choice, we ain't got a choice.

Just start over somewhere?

That was the plan all along, wasn't it?

Maybe it was your plan, Beau. I don't recall ever being asked.

Well, look, we ain't got time for this. Pack up as much as we can carry—canned food, matches, and whatever personals you think you need. And tell Cal to pack up—

He's asleep.

He's asleep?

He said he was tired and he went off to bed.

Fine. Let him sleep. We'll wake him up in a few hours and he can pack then.

I'll put some clothes up for him.

Do that. I'm gonna get the goods from under the house and pack up the weapons.

You do that.

When they were done, there were a few bags full of cash, beanie weenie, and Beau's small arsenal stacked across the sofa. The two adults stood at the kitchen counter, drinking beers.

Let's go to bed, he said.

What for?

You know what for.

What is *wrong* with you?

What're you talkin' bout?

You want to fuck at a time like this?

It's as good a time as any.

How do you figure that?

We got thirty minutes before we gotta get Cal up, and we ain't gonna be doing much of anything between us while we're up in that one-room-shack with maybe four other couples and all their kids between 'em.

She sipped her Lone Star and stared at the fridge door—her son's drawings and the grizzly bear magnet he'd made her out of popsicle sticks and dry macaroni for Mother's Day three years earlier.

You tellin' me a good screwing wouldn't clear some of the anxiety out of your mind, too?

She scowled up at him.

He was handsome. His hair flicked indifferently across his brow. Broad shoulders and biceps the size of softballs.

Before either of them had a chance to think, they were in the bedroom, tearing at each other's clothes. He fumbled with her bra as she fumbled with his belt buckle. They kissed and nipped and pushed and shoved until they were somewhat naked—naked enough—and flopped down on the old mattress whose springs squeaked under their weight. She wasn't her usual self—there was no shouting, there were no boisterous moans—in their place were panting and carnal grunts. Her nails were dug into his back and he was nearly finished when, through the pulse of blood vessels he heard the sound of a motorbike pull up the street. He stopped his motion and sat up enough to glance out the window. A rider pulled into their lot and parked next to his truck. As the tall figure walked under the gleam of the sodium lamp overhead, Beau instantly recognized the Mexican teen he'd nearly beaten earlier that day.

Instinctively, he fumbled on a pair of shorts, stuffed his pistol down the back, and approached the kitchen window. The teen was standing about, nervously. He made a move toward the front door, then backed away and around in a circle across the grass.

Beau flung the door open and was down the stairs in one bound.

You want more, son?

Mr. Moreland, the teen looked up quickly.

His voice was small. Beau stopped in his tracks. His arms felt like lead again.

What?

I'm sorry to intrude, sir—I know it's late, but I saw all your lights on and thought maybe we could talk.

T—Talk? Beau stammered.

The teen nodded.

What about?

I wanted to apologize for what happened between us.

Wait—to apologize to *me*?

Yes, sir.

For what?

You see, sir, when I came up here, my cousin James told me about you.

What'd old James have to say?

He said you were a veteran. And a decorated one at that.

What about it?

Well, sir, I've been thinking about joining the armed forces, but I can't decide between Marines and Army, and James said you might be a person I could learn from that might help me make the right decision.

Beau felt his head roll toward his right shoulder.

But the first time I saw you, sir, you looked at me real funny. And I thought maybe you didn't like Chicanos. I thought maybe you were racist.

What's your name, son?

Julio.

I'm not prejudice, Julio. I had some other things on my mind.

I understand. And that's why I wanted to apologize. I let my own preconception get in the way of approaching you, and I think I might have even goaded you on, because, I had lost respect for you.

Beau looked toward the grass at his bare feet.

Then I heard from my grandma that you fixed her fence and didn't even charge her nothing. I thought, damn, that's the kind of man I want to be. So, I came up here to apologize because I shouldn't have judged you without even knowing you.

Julio, I'm the one who should—

A sound from his past interrupted his thought. His mind took an aeon to process what in a flash his senses beheld—a bang and a blaze and the young man in front of him spun to the green earth. Bells rang for an instant and then all he could hear was his own labored breathing. Then, in a rush of adrenaline, all of his instincts and training came flooding back to him.

He ran and knelt beside Julio and took him in his arms. The teen's dark eyes blinked rapidly as blood pulsed from his gaping neck with every beat of his heart. Beau looked down to see such carnage as he hadn't witnessed since he'd left Qui Nhon in a helicopter. His eyes searched the yards all around him intuitively, but he saw nothing save bedroom lights flipping on as his neighbors began to survey the situation by which they'd been awakened.

Beau turned to his right to see Cal at the top step, smoking shotgun in his hands.

No—no!

The gun slipped limply from his fingers as the boy's face betrayed the terror in his soul.

Cal—God—*no!*

Then, Annabelle was at the door behind the boy. She screamed when she saw the mangled corpse in her husband's arms. Beau stared down as the Mexican's body violently shuttered its last, then peered past the dingy haze above him and toward the luminous specks that were Jupiter and Venus. If he'd have mistaken one or the other for Mars at that moment he might be forgiven.

Another presence came into focus—that of Julio's cousin James, standing at the edge of the driveway. Beau's head jolted back and forth as any attempt at words failed him. James backed toward his motorbike slowly, hopped on, and revved off down the street and out of sight. A crowd of neighbors began to appear, their audible gasps piercing the silence around him. Beau held Julio's slack remains to his chest while his shotgun reposed at his son's small feet.

*Fin.*

# CAMINO REAL

"Santi, your padre was a bad man."

Looking out over the sprawling and arid llanura to the south, he remained silent.

"You understand me?"

"Sí."

"Your padre was a *very* bad man."

"Sí."

"You must make penance for his soul, if you wish him to be delivered from purgatory."

"What if I do not wish this?"

"It is your duty as a son."

"He was not much of a padre."

"It is still your duty."

"He left me in the orphanage when I was six, even though he was still alive then."

"You must make penance for his soul. It is your sacred duty."

"Not if he was not mi padre—"

"The book says," the priest slammed his plump fingers on the church's registry, "he is your padre. And *god* says it is your duty to make penance for his soul."

"But he was baptized."

"He was a *sinner*."

"Are we not all sinners?"

"Some are worse than others, and your padre was among the worst."

"Does god not have mercy?"

"Not on sinners—on sinners, only justice."

"This does not seem just."

"Your padre refused confession. He refused penance. He was not eligible for absolution or last rites."

"Who decides he was not eligible?"

"The priest. He did not confess. He is not absolved."

"Does the rain not fall on the just and the unjust alike?"

"Stop arguing—it is not your place."

Santi looked calmly toward the last rays of the setting sun over the ridge.

"If you do not make the Pilgrimage of Sinners on behalf of your padre, you put your own soul and the souls of your niños in peril as well."

"How is this so?"

"If you do not have mercy on the soul of your padre, the sinner, god will not have mercy on your soul, and your niños will bear the burden of your inconstancy."

"I am to have mercy on the soul of a sinner, but god will not?"

"I will have no more of this blasphemy. You put your soul and the souls of your niños in peril."

"Then I will go. And I will make penance."

"Good. It is your duty."

The fleshy old priest lurched forward and pushed himself out of his throne-like armchair. He shuffled over to the bookcase and opened the cabinet. He dusted off a folded booklet and handed it to Santi.

"Seven churches or holy sites. Two pesos you must donate at each stop to receive a stamp. When you have made all your donations, completed your acts of penance, and received all your stamps, you bring this book back to me, and I will issue your padre a certificate of absolution. Then we pray that god has mercy on his soul."

"Two pesos at seven sites?"

"Si."

"I paid mi padre's debts already. I only make sixty pesos per año."

"Then you must sell your possessions. Are the souls of your padre and your niños worth so little to you?"

Santi opened the booklet and glanced at the map inside.

"This is nearly five-hundred miles—it will take *weeks*. Who will provide for my family during this time?"

"This is not my concern. My concern is the stamps. You make your donations and collect the stamps, and I will do my best to absolve your padre, the sinner."

"This is god's mercy?"

"This is why you should not die a sinner. Do not burden god, or your family, in such a fashion after you are gone."

Santi began to rise from his knees.

"Let me bless your journey first, mi hijo."

The young man knelt back down with a roll of his eyes.

"May god bless and keep you, give you steady feet, and protection. And may you not deviate from the pilgrimage as it is prescribed in the Book of the Saints, that you may indeed rectify this unfortunate debt which your padre, *the sinner*, owes to the church and to god."

The priest rubbed sacred oil on Santi's forehead in the shape of the passion with his fat thumb.

"And may you not forget to make your donation to this church when you arrive home safely. Now, you may rise and may god's peace be upon you."

He turned his back on Santi and left him alone in the registry room. The pilgrim rose to his feet as oil dripped down his nose. He wiped it away with his sleeve. As he stood to leave, he glanced at the table that housed the registry book of the town. He flipped its massive leather cover open and turned the yellowed pages until he found his padre's last name. He scanned down through his paternal lineage—tenant farmers mostly, the occasional fisherman or cattle driver mixed in—all faithful to the church until his padre. Iñigo Vidal Bustos—date of death, May 14, 1937. Santi heard a noise in the next room and closed the book suddenly before seeing the details of his padre's unconfessed sin.

He walked through the rounded archways and out into the fading sun. He watched silently as the sepultureros lowered his padre's wooden casket into the yawning pauper's grave, the last of the paid mourners' artificial wailing and weeping dying with the light.

He stopped and picked some wildflowers on the way home and met his wife, Ana, at the door of the one-room, mud-brick home. She smiled warmly and wrapped her arms around his shoulders. The children were sleeping already.

"What did Padre César say?"

"That mi padre was unconfessed, and that I must make the Pilgrimage of Sinners on behalf of his soul."

Her cheeks became taut and her black eyes brimmed with tears.

"Do not cry, mi amor," he said as he gently caressed her cheek. "I will sell the bicicleta and the motor. That should be enough to cover the donations and provide for you and los niños while I am gone. You will have the pollos, too."

"Do not sell the motor. You have worked on it for six months."

"I can build another when I return."

"Sell mi madre's necklace instead," she pleaded, touching the string of pearls around her long, graceful neck.

"I could never do that."

"Please, you will need the motor to plow the fields during harvest."

"I have plowed fields by hand my whole life. I am still but thirty-three. One more year will not break me."

"But your motor—and your bicicleta. You love your bicicleta. Mi madre's pearls would bring more than the bicicleta and the motor both, with some left over, probably."

"I won't sell your madre's pearls. They are your pearls now, and I could not bear the shame if they belonged to a woman who was not as worthy of them as you."

"Mi amor, how long will you be gone?"

"Five weeks, I think."

"Five weeks?"

"Sí."

"But the baby may be here before then."

He glanced down at her swollen belly and touched his palm to it softly.

"Your hermana and her esposo must come."

"I will ask."

"He can help with the animals, and she can help if the baby comes."

"Sí."

"Good."

"Santi?"

"Sí?"

"Do you believe the priest?"

"Believe what?"

"That your padre was a sinner?"

"Sí."

"Do you believe that your act of penance on his behalf will be enough to earn his pardon?"

"I suppose."

"It seems like a lot of trouble if you don't truly believe."

"It seems like a lot of trouble to ask a man to leave his family, sell his belongings, and risk his life for a padre who abandoned him."

"Oh, Santi, what if you don't come home?"

"I will come home. You must believe that."

Her eyes suddenly darted toward the ceiling. She spun on her nimble bare feet and rushed toward the cupboard. She knelt down on the dirt floor and pulled the curtain back.

"Ana?"

"Si?"

"What are you looking for?"

She rummaged through blankets and bowls and linens and then emerged with a delicate silver chalice. She brought it to her husband with great care.

"Where did you get that?"

"It was mi tío abuelo's."

"But what is it?"

"A *chalice*."

"Do you want to sell it?"

"No, no—of course not."

His dumbfounded look turned from the chalice to her dark eyes.

"Then what?"

"Between Chalendo and Andachuo, there is a monastery—the Blessed Monasterio of the work of San Francisco de Monterata. You must go there."

"Monterata? That's dozens of miles out of the way!"

"You *must* go there, Santi."

"Why on earth?"

"Mi tío abuelo walked the Pilgrimage of Sinners on behalf of his cousin, who was an unconfessed thief."

"I did not know this."

"He was climbing the path through the mountain pass in early spring and was blown off-course by a late season snow storm. He found his way through a narrow valley lined with banyan trees. He sustained himself on bananas and roots and came over a ridge and through a clearing into the great valley of Monterata. He approached the great monasterio, where he was given this chalice."

She held the delicately engraved silver cup to his eye level. It was magnificent—unlike any cup he'd ever seen. It was the kind of grail he'd watched royalty sip from in the dreams of his childhood long ago.

"So why do I have to go there?"

"A monk at the monasterio gave him a magical potion to drink—a sacred, miraculous potion brewed in secret behind the walls of the monasterio. The monk told him it would cure all kinds of ills and provide a boundary of protection all around him. The monk then gave him the chalice to drink from. Mi tío abuelo came home safely after that, like a man glowing with the light of the sun, and did not even have blisters on his feet. And he lived until he was more than one hundred years old."

"And did he complete the Pilgrimage?"

She paused and looked off into the distance as if the memory were written on the horizon.

"You know, I can't tell you that he did."

"He never told you?"

"I don't think he did. In fact, I barely remember hearing him speak of the pilgrimage at all. He only spoke of Monterata."

"Well, I don't know if it's such a good idea. I already am not sure I believe in the pilgrimage altogether. I'm sure I don't believe in magical potions or secret monasterios. And also, Padre César specifically told me not to leave the path."

"Mi amor, god will not count against you a diversion to a blessed and sacred place. In fact, the added distance only adds to the penance you pay. Surely this act of faithfulness will only count in your favor when judgement comes."

"Why do you insist that I go so far out of the way? This will add maybe weeks to my journey—and you and los niños will be without me even longer. There is no doubt you would have the baby before I returned."

"I will have the baby in your absence. But only if you go to Monterata and drink the potion can I be sure that you will return home safely to me."

"This is a much heavier burden on my shoulders, Ana."

"It will greatly ease my burden, Santi. *Por favor.*"

"Ok. I will leave the path and drink of the potion at Monterata. Only to please you, mi amor."

She kissed him ardently and trembled in his arms.

That night, they made love gently and eagerly on their small cot in the corner and slept warm and satisfied in each others arms.

The next day, Santi sold the bicicleta to Luis Gomez, the town's butcher, and the motor to Juan Bragada, the owner of the adjoining land—and for probably less than it was worth. He also sold various trinkets, tools in disrepair, and even a couple old sows. He bought some extra wool socks in the village, along with a resoled pair of boots, which he would bring in the event that his fell into disrepair on the journey. He gave the shoemaker a bushel of maiz and a couple dozen huevos in exchange for the boots. In all, he was prepared to leave his wife and niños with seven pesos, and to take eighteen with him on his journey—fourteen for the donations, and the other four for expenses he might incur.

He spent the following night in candlelight, drawing out a detailed map of the path he would walk. Sixty miles to the Church of San Marino at Concurra. Eighty miles from there to the sacred shrine of Don Mentiroso at Huerchito. Another sixty or so to the Church of Heavy Shoulders at Chalendo. Then, forty-seven miles, from what he could gather, through the mountain pass to Monterata. From there, ninety miles back on the path to the fourth church at Andachuo. Forty miles to La Capilla de Santa Maria de La Paz, one hundred-fifteen miles to the shrine at Rio Martes, fifty miles to La Caverna de los Misterios Grande, and roughly one-hundred and twenty miles home.

For the next two days, Ana fed him tortillas and huevos, strong peppers, and horchata, along with a heavy dose of love, to fortify him for the journey. He read to his niños until they fell asleep. He packed his bag with his good knife, canteen, a couple packs of matches, a small cast-iron skillet, his extra socks and boots, a second pair of warm pants, his winter poncho, and the food Ana had prepared for his journey. He put the guidebook and map inside the canvas bag he would sling over his shoulders.

She kissed the bowl of the chalice fervently before placing it gently in his bag.

"Do not forsake the monasterio, Santi, for me."

"I will not," he answered.

He kissed his niños goodbye as they slept, and then embraced his wife. She clung to him so tightly that he wasn't sure he had the strength to leave her. They kissed as if they would never see each other again.

"It's alright," she said, finally breaking their grasp. "Mi hermana and her esposo will be here this afternoon. And you will be back in six weeks, mi amor. I will pray over you constantly."

"I love you, Ana," he said with a final kiss.

He gathered his pack and left the house, looking back over his shoulder a few houses down the road to see her standing in the threshold, waving delicately.

Santi did what he could to keep his emotions intact—to hold himself together, for that matter. His thoughts hadn't been consumed by the magnitude of the pilgrimage while he had still been with her. But now, the sight of her fading in the distance between them, the enormity of the task was suddenly obvious. He wiped his eyes with the backs of his hands as he mounted the small hill that led through the center of town toward the church where his journey would officially begin.

He was somewhat surprised to see a small crowd gathered in the courtyard as he approached. A small town, the crowd was composed entirely of people he knew—some of whom he had known his entire life—including Luis Gomez, Juan Bragada, and of course, Padre César. With the Book of the Saints cupped in one hand, and an enormous gold medallion around his neck, it was the priest's long black frock that gave Santi a chill—almost as if he was attending another funeral, perhaps his own this time. The priest waved him near, and he was taken aback by the jeering faces of in crowd—formerly friendly faces turned to scowls and snarls.

"Mi hijo," the swarthy priest bellowed. "Bow before me, as I again bless your journey."

Santi reluctantly kneeled and immediately felt a rush of nerves as the crowd pressed in around him.

"May our loving father of all grace and mercy wash you clean of all of your transgressions, your filth, and your inner darkness, which would otherwise consume you. May you, as precious oro is purified by only the fiercest inferno, be so purified in soul, that the loving father may once again deign to look upon you. May, through the suffering of a servant—nay, a *sinner*—you obtain peace for the soul of your most wicked padre. And may you, though you have a thorn which thus embattles your flesh, in the spirit of San Pablo himself, complete your journey devoid of pride, humanity, and rebellion."

The priest made the sign of the passion over him. Luis Gomez stepped out of the crowd and hit Santi with a piece of iron pipe, across his ribcage, just under his outstretched arm. He crumpled face down in the dirt and heaved for air.

"And now," the holy man continued, "that you have obtained a thorn in your flesh, be rid of you! Be rid of you, sinner! Our loving father is too holy to look upon such filth—as are we, a holy people! Be gone!"

The mob began shouting and set upon him. He was being kicked and stomped from every angle. His instincts took over as he scrambled to his feet and began to run. He felt rocks pelt his back and the back of his head—one even cut him just over his ear. The angry shouts and accusations began to fade to silence as he stumbled his way down the dirt road that would eventually lead him to Concurra. Eventually, his gait slowed, and he began to feel sick. He sat down in the dust and looked back over his village, church spires dominating the landscape. He lifted his shirt and saw a deep blood bruise rising to the surface on his left side. He panted heavily and cringed as he touched it with his fingers. He tried to convince himself that nothing was broken, but he had his doubts. After sipping some water from his flask, he stood and began again.

The rest of the day was less eventful. He stopped to rest every three miles or so, ate a few tortillas, and said prayers over his esposa and his niños. He also managed a prayer for the soul of his padre.

Having covered what must have been close to twenty-five miles, he came upon a small village, not unlike his own. He paid a sixty centavos for a crude dinner and a cot in a barn. He was, however, thankful that the night was so calm and balmy, as the fleas forced him to sleep under the stars. In the morning, the "innkeeper" refused him a refund, but was eventually talked into providing a breakfast of beans and peppers and fresh water from the nearby well, by way of apology.

The second day of his journey was, perhaps, the hottest day of the year to that point. The sun sweltered overhead as he trudged the dusty and open terrain, heading south. It was during this day that he began to feel the blisters on his feet. Around noon, he switched to his new pair of boots, thinking he might break them in easier if he only used them a half-day at a time. The pain was nearly unbearable, causing his eyes to well and his teeth to clench with each step. He was disappointed to only conquer perhaps fifteen miles that day, due in large part to the blisters. He set up camp in a sparse grove of trees that might provide some shelter during the night, and built a small fire on which to cook a few huevos. He took his socks off to discover that they were nearly soaked through with blood. He poured some water on them, and his feet, to try to clean them, almost immediately regretting the action, as water was his most precious and limited resource.

It seemed that the drop in temperature corresponded directly with the drop of the sun on the horizon. He shivered all night under his poncho and awoke feeling like his throat was raw. He tried to sip some water, but it was useless. He pulled his scratchy socks up over his chafed feet and packed up camp. The purple bruise on his ribcage had spread down to the top of his thigh. He watched with concern as his orange-colored urine splashed some roots and a small ant hill. He forced some water down his throat and spat out phlegm before starting back down the road.

The path cut awkwardly through a dense patch of fiddlewood trees and over a ridge. The angle of his stride caused by the steep incline introduced Santi's feet to a whole new level of pain. He climbed slowly and cautiously as the beaten path narrowed with overgrowth and vines. Scurried footsteps momentarily alarmed him as some small and unseen critters fled his movement. Although his pace was slow and his walking difficult, he was thankful to be out of the direct sunlight for what turned into several hours. Birds of all colors and sizes squawked as their wings fluttered through the narrow strips of sunlight overhead. His saving grace for the day was that the vigorous activity seemed numb his throat to a tolerable threshold. He ate a small lunch and rested under a chaya tree and picked a good supply of its leaves for use in his dinner that night. He changed his boots again, as well as his socks, and headed out.

After another hour or so, the terrain leveled out, and the grove became more sparse. As he followed the path around a sharp curve, he began to hear what sounded like voices in the distance—cheerful voices, full of laughter. He rounded the bend, and the trees gave way to a clearing that opened to a small village surrounded by a ten-foot wall painted pink. A church sat in the city center, surrounded by dozens of homes and bustling shops. Santi watched with fascination as a bevy of niños parted in two for incoming cars and a motorbike. As he neared the pedestrian gate, the niños kicked their gray leather ball in his direction. Santi instinctively kicked it back, and then unleashed a howl of pain from his blistered foot. The niños laughed joyfully and then swarmed him with shouts and questions. He spoke gruffly, trying not to irritate his throat, and asked where he might find water. They led him by the hand through the gate and down narrow streets and even narrower alleys, and all with glee and mirth. The buildings themselves were painted all different colors of the rainbow and seemed to radiate happiness and warmth. The niños brought their new friend to a fountain in the courtyard at the center of town, the Church of San Marino, just across the plaza.

"This is Concurra?" Santi asked.

"Si! Si!"

"Thank god," he replied before dunking his head in the cool, clean water.

The niños shrieked with excitement and surprise. Santi came up out of the fountain refreshed and chuckling. He rubbed his sore eyes and brushed the water from his hair with his hands.

"Niños, do you know where I can find some food?"

"Si! Si!"

They took him by the hand again and practically pulled him across the way to a small cafe where he ate barbacoa and drank agua fresca, while his devoted and cheerful following sat outside on the ledge. The meal cost him forty centavos.

"Niños, what is the name of the Padre in the church?"

"Padre Miguel!" they answered in unison.

"Simple enough. Thank you."

He stretched his arms to the sky until his back popped audibly, which gave the young people yet another reason to bellow in laughter. He gathered his things and thanked them again for their help, before crossing the plaza toward the church. It was painted in the same glowing and sanguine pink as the wall that surrounded what had turned out to be a most pleasant town.

Santi was greeted at the door by an elderly nun named Isabella and taken down a tiled hall to the padre's study, where he was asked to wait. He sat down gently and savored the sensation of the cushioned leather guest-chair on his weary backside. The furniture in the room was dark and constructed from rich wood—maybe even imported wood. There were piles of books, rosaries, and papers scattered about, as well as what looked to be a change of clothes on a hanger near the window.

Santi was not impatient to leave the comfortable and cool surroundings of Padre Miguel's study. However, the shooting pain in his side reminded him that this would not be a pleasant journey, and that he needed to expect much hardship in the coming days. He was almost anxious for his business to be over in the church so that he could spend the night in such a pleasant town and in such pleasant company as the people of Concurra.

Just then, the heavy door creaked loudly on its hinges, and a sprightly man in his mid-thirties entered. He was thin and dark-haired and had an enthusiastic spring in his step—the complete opposite of Padre César.

"Hello, pilgrim," he said as he moved briskly to put out his hand. Santi tried with some effort to stand to his feet before he was politely asked not to rise. "You must be exhausted."

"Sí."

The young priest casually leaned against his desk.

"What is the distance between your home and here—it must be at least fifty miles?"

"Sixty."

"Whew," the young priest shook his head and whistled. "Well, it is obvious that you are a good pilgrim. I understand that it is on behalf of your padre's soul that you take the Pilgrimage of Sinners?"

"Si."

"Mmm," he nodded thoughtfully. "Do you know the sins that your father committed that were unconfessed to the church?"

"No."

"Very serious," he began slowly. "Very serious transgressions, indeed."

Santi shrugged. What they were made no difference—they had put him on this path, and that was all that mattered to him.

"And you are a faithful church member?"

"Si."

"And your children have been baptized?"

"Si."

"Very good," Padre Miguel answered with a warm smile. "It is important to root out any evils in your family line and rectify them going forward, no?"

"Si."

"Si."

The priest stood and poured himself a drink.

"Have you had something to drink?"

"Si."

"Water, I hope?"

"Si—and agua fresca."

"Good," he answered, while taking a sip of his brandy-colored drink. "You are aware that the consumption of alcohol is strictly forbidden to pilgrims?"

"Si."

"Good. I hope you don't mind that I indulge in your presence, then."

Santi just shrugged his shoulders. Who was he to tell a padre what he could eat or drink?

The young priest breathed deeply, then set his glass down on the desk in front of him. He opened a drawer and from it pulled a black box made of some kind of metal. On its lid was a lock. He fumbled inside his frock for a key ring and then unlocked the box.

"I assume you have your donation with you?"

"Si," Santi said, plucking two pesos from his bag. He leaned forward and handed them over the desk to the priest.

"Just—just put them in here," Padre Miguel directed. "It is best that I do not handle it directly."

Santi dropped the cash into the slot in the top of the box.

"It's god's money now," the priest said as he closed the box and locked it again. "It will do much good in this community. Thank you."

"Do I get my stamp now?"

"Your stamp? Oh, no, you do not receive the stamp in exchange for the donation. You must commit an act of penance."

"Perdóname?"

"Penance. You must complete an act of penance in order to receive the stamp."

"Is not this pilgrimage an act of penance?"

"To some degree, yes, but individual acts of penance will be required at each stop—starting here."

Santi groaned—in part because of a sharp pain in his side, in part because of this newly added dimension to his trip.

"And what is this act of penance? Must I chant or say a certain number of prayers?"

"Something like that. Leave your things here. Follow me."

With reluctance, Santi rose and followed Padre Miguel through the door and then down the hall toward the rear of the church. The priest opened the back door and held it for the pilgrim to pass through.

Down a few steps, Santi looked out over an open courtyard, much like the one out front, the only difference being that here, a pillory stood in place of the fountain. Santi closed his eyes in disbelief.

"How long?"

"Twenty-four hours."

"What if I refuse?"

"You put your padre's soul in eternal peril, not to mention the souls of your niños."

"It will be a cold night—maybe even frost."

"If it was easy, it wouldn't be penance."

With that, the priest snapped his fingers toward two men, previously unnoticed by Santi, standing across the way under a canvas tarp. They were gruff and dirty looking. They took the pilgrim roughly by the arms and forced him down the steps and put his head and his arms through the holes and locked the post down on him. He stood helpless and exposed, facing the town and cursing his padre. The two men removed his boots and bloody socks, then walked slowly and calmly back to their original position in the shade and leaned back against the wall of the building across the street. The sun was beginning its descent and a northernly wind was beginning to pick up. Santi stood in silence, breathing laboriously, watching townsfolk pass and glare at him—some in surprise, some out of contempt. Initially, there were just a few stragglers here and there, but as time went on, people began to gather in front of him en masse.

As the cluster became thicker and more densely packed, Santi heard the church door swing open behind him again. Footsteps approached and stopped. After most of the people in the crowd bowed and made the sign of the passion, the priest began to address them.

"This man," he started. "This man, is representative of a sinner's soul, unconfessed and unreconciled to the church of god."

The people raised their fists in righteous anger and scowled at him. Some of the children who led him so joyfully around the city that very day snuck to the front of the crowd and jeered.

"This man," Padre Miguel continued, "deserves our pity, yes, but he deserves our attention even more. He serves as a reminder to us all and to our niños, not to stray from the path so mercifully laid out before us by god our father and his church. This man is the living embodiment of the worst kind of sinner—the unrepentant, profligate, degenerate, and depraved sinner—who not only deserves the humiliation he receives, but also deserves our wrath, on behalf of our loving and just god."

The crowd cheered at this—the jubilant laughter of the children replaced by the agitated taunts of the sanctimonious. Padre Miguel crossed directly in front of Santi, quieted the crowd, and then turned to face him. He mumbled some sort of prayer while he dabbed sacred oil on the pilgrim's forehead.

He then crossed back behind Santi and out of his field of vision. The pilgrim watched the eyes of the mob and waited for whatever would come next. He thought he heard fabric being discarded behind him, then, the priest crossed once more in front of him—black frock shed to reveal a clean white shirt, sleeves rolled to the elbows. In his hand was rolled a leather whip.

"This, mi hijo, is for the purification of your soul."

"No, no," Santi shouted as the crowd began to roar.

The priest lifted the pilgrims shirt over the bar of the stock. Santi gritted his teeth in expectation of the first blow. The crowd grew louder and louder, more and more raucous—almost as if the priest was egging them on. Out of the corner of his eye, he caught a glimpse of a gray object hurtling in his direction. He instinctively yanked his neck to move his head out of the object's direct trajectory, but was prevented by the wood stock. The rotten cabbage hit the plank directly to his right and nearly exploded, covering his hair and his nose in putrid mush. He spit and did his best to shake it off his head as the mass of onlookers roared in approval. The next instant, a sudden whooshing sound was halted by the smack of his flesh. Santi crumpled as far as the pillory would allow him. The assembly again thundered its approval. Another thwack against his exposed back, then another and another, his warm blood running down his legs inside of his pants. He wasn't sure how many times he was hit before blacking out, but he remembered coming to for a few moments to the terror of the mob surrounding him, spitting and slapping and kicking him. He was particularly heartbroken by the memory of those children, bottom lips pursed in a hateful scowl, pulling clumps of his hair out with their bare hands.

When he came to, it was dark, save a single torch burning on a stake across the plaza. He was still pinned to the pillory, although the crowd was gone and he seemed to be alone. The wind was biting and, although he was exceedingly sore all over, he couldn't help but shiver. He thought his shirt might be frozen to the fluids on his back but, in reality, had no idea. He gingerly shifted his weight onto one foot, the blisters making him wonder if he was standing in a pile of broken glass. He heard himself moan softly. He also realized that he had, at some point, defecated on himself. This was the shame of a sinner, he supposed. He wouldn't wish it on his worst enemy.

Santi was unable to sleep and watched the sun take an eternity to rise. He was thankful for its warmth as it peered over the rooftops and ridges to his east. In a matter of an hour or so, however, he was baking. His throat was sore and caked dry. The happy town bustled on in seeming ignorance to his presence, to his plight. He managed to croak out a request for water to several passersby, who avoided his glance with obvious intent, skittering about to their destinations in willful disregard. As the day went on, he felt the urge to urinate, but was unable to attract anyone's notice. Childlike shame enveloped him as he felt his warm waste run down his legs and settle around his burning feet.

Finally, after what can only be described as an aeon, Padre Miguel emerged from the church behind him with the two ruffians who had locked him in the pillory the previous day. The lock clicked and the wood board lifted from his head. Santi collapsed in the mix of dust, blood, and bodily waste. He clutched his side and his back and gasped for air.

"Mi hijo, look at me," the priest sternly commanded.

Santi craned his neck with some effort, his eyes having trouble finding focus on the young padre's face in the glare of the sun.

"You have finished your penance. Your book has been stamped. Now you must go."

Santi's eyes fell to the earth before him.

"You must go."

"Now?"

"Si. You bear the sin of the dead. And our people send you out into the wilderness, god-willing, bearing whatever sin lives in our midst. You are our scapegoat."

"Agua, por favor?"

"No. You are too full of sin for a holy people to gaze upon."

Santi's belongings were tossed in a heap in the dust.

"Now be gone, and may the peace of god be upon you."

The pilgrim gathered his things and clawed himself unsteadily to his feet.

"These men will escort you to the gate. You will continue south to Huerchito, where you will visit the Shrine of Don Mentiroso and continue your attempt to make peace with our loving and just god."

Santi nodded and shuffled delicately in the direction the men pointed him.

"And thank you for your donation," Padre Miguel called over Santi's shoulder. The pilgrim stopped in his tracks. If he wasn't beaten and bruised, he might have fought the man. But who was he to fight a padre?

He received a rough shove at the town gate and stumbled forward, his wife's chalice rolling out of his bag into the dirt. He quickly chased after it and brushed it off. Looking up, he noticed a group of children who had frozen like statues in the middle of their game. They glared intensely at him—some with terror, some with spite. He collected his things again, stood, and began to trudge off to the south along the dirt road. In something like half a mile, behind the cover of a thick line of bushes, he disrobed and attempted to beat the excrement out of his pants. He had to peel his shirt from his flesh, and glanced over his shoulder to observe what he could of his ravaged back. He did his best to brush himself off, put on new clothes, along with fresh socks and boots, and started off down the path again. His pace was slow and labored, his pain intense, and his thirst wretchedly unquenched. He reached in his satchel to discover that his huevos and matches were gone. He was tentatively surprised, however, that he was still in possession of his knife, pan, and poncho. The path was mostly uncovered, and the sun was a brutal tyrant. He was thankful, however, for the small mercy of mostly flat terrain.

In a few hours time, he came upon another rather dense patch of fiddlewood trees. His ears perked to a strange sound—a rustling, whirling sound. The path had been overtaken by brush, so much so that he struggled mightily to claw through it. The sound got louder the closer he got. With a few grunts and hacks with his knife, he cut a hole through the brush and looked out over a marvelous and shady clearing, a rushing stream down below. The shock of it was nearly too much to take in, and his mind instantly reminded him that many weary travelers had made the mistake of believing they had found an oasis like this, only to despair as their hands and mouths pressed into nothing but hot sand.

He cautiously descended the bank, his ears set ablaze by the sound of the water, a sound so beautiful, he thought it might only be compared to the first whimpers of his children at birth, or the sound of his wife's impassioned breathing as they made love. He slid down the last few feet of the rim and then crawled, mad with hope, to the edge of the stream. He dipped an index finger in, and sure enough, the water was cold and clean. He lapped it desperately and nearly choked with laughter after his first few big gulps. In an instant his clothes were off and he was submerged in it. It was then that, for the first time, his eyes took in the insurmountable beauty all around him—hundreds of plumeria flowers ablaze in the glow of the setting sun, passion flowers, and star fruit hanging all around. It was also while taking all of these exotic sights and smells in that his eyes fell upon a group of men sitting across the bank not thirty feet from him. After the initial shock, his heart sank to his blistered toes. By their clothing, posture, and open display of weaponry, he could tell beyond a shadow of a doubt—they were bandidos, and they had been watching him. He had no idea what to do.

"Hello," he called out.

"Bueno," the one with the tattoo on his face called back.

"I'm sorry for disturbing your camp," Santi called.

"You don't disturb us," the dark one called with a chuckle. "You have been quite the entertainer."

Santi looked down at the rushing water and then back to the gangsters on the far bank.

"Is it ok if I gather my things and leave?"

"What things do you have to gather?"

"Nothing much, just a bag and some dirty clothes."

"Well then, gather your things."

"Gracias," he replied, quite relieved, but still under the expectation of being robbed and beaten again. He climbed the embankment stark naked and began clothing himself.

"You've had quite the ordeal, from what I can see," the tattooed one called.

Santi simply nodded and put a clean shirt over his head.

"It's a shame," the one with the sombrero bellowed.

The pilgrim had his things and turned back toward the thieves across the river. Bravery—or insanity—overtook him.

"May I wash a set of clothes and fill up a canteen?"

"Why do you ask our permission? Do we own el río?"

"I just," he started with some hesitation. "I just wasn't sure if I would be disturbing you."

"We already told you that you don't bother us. Are you thick?"

He shook his head and thanked them. He proceeded to fill his water and wash his soiled clothing as best he could, keeping his head down as a show of humility. He thanked them again once he finished and began to trace the path downstream.

"Where are you going?" the big one with the huge scar on his chest asked.

"From here, to Huerchito."

"Huerchito?"

"Si."

"That's quite a distance."

"Si."

"And it's already almost dark. Aren't you afraid you'll get robbed?"

"I suppose it could happen. But there is nothing for anyone to rob from me."

"Ha!" the dark one burst out. "There is always something to rob—always."

The others chuckled, faces twisted into terrifying shadows around their fire.

"Do you intend to rob me?" Santi asked. "I would gladly give you anything I have, as long as you let me free with no harm."

The dark one stood and nearly pounced down to the riverbank, separated from the pilgrim only by the narrow stream.

"You mistake our meaning," he barked. "I apologize if we're not educated in the ways of cultured society. We were trying to ask you to eat with us."

Santi nearly fell down dead on the spot.

"You don't intend to rob me?"

"You are a pilgrim, no?"

"Si."

"We do not rob pilgrims. It's bad luck."

He waved Santi across, and after brief introductions, the traveler found himself eating pollo and beans and rice. He was even offered what smelled like tequila, which he declined. There were about eight bandidos in all, and Santi liked every one of them. He slept soundly that night and was awoken only by stirring in the camp. He immediately reached for his bag and was somewhat surprised that its contents were all as he'd left them.

"If you wish to pack up now, we can take you through until the forest clears out. It's about five miles, and pretty dangerous unless you have an escort. There are bandidos that don't have the same religious sensitivities as us."

"Thank you for your kindness."

"De nada."

The men decamped and trotted down to the path. In what he figured was almost exactly five miles, the trees thinned out and opened onto a barren and seemingly endless llanura. The one with the tattoo handed Santi an extra canteen along with a bag full of fruit and simply said, "You're going to need this."

"The only thing between here and Huerchito is a little village called Árido," the dark one said. "That's about thirty-five miles. Do not stop until you get there. Do not even rest. Do you understand me?"

Santi nodded sullenly.

"You must not stop, ok?"

"Sí."

"Spend the night there, fill up on water, and then on to Huerchito, another twenty-five or so miles. Again, once you leave Árido, do not stop for a moment, even to rest."

"Ok."

"There are snakes, too—big snakes—and scorpions. If you get bit by a black one, it will hurt like hell, but you'll live. If you get bit by a red one, you will soon join your ancestors in purgatory, ok?"

"Sí."

"You get bit by a red one, you'll be dead in an hour."

"Ok."

"And remember—do not stop."

"Sí. Gracias."

"De nada, mi compa. Adiós."

In an instant, the bandidos were submerged again in the jungle, their movements out of sight and even earshot. Santi braced himself, thought of his Ana, his niños, and his padre, said a prayer, and started out into the desert. The sun was still low as he set out, and he was resolved to get as many miles in as he could before it rose to full force. The path was marked through the desert by stakes sticking up three to six feet, depending on the depth of the sand. Despite his deteriorated physical condition, he made good progress, and by his count, had walked nearly ten miles by noon. He sipped some water and ate a piece of guava as he walked, not stopping for even a brief moment.

At around three that afternoon, some clouds rolled in from the west, bringing an astounding amount of relief in the form of shade. However, with the clouds came the wind, which began as a breeze and escalated to a gale. Santi did his best to shield his eyes as he pressed on. After a few minutes of the howling storm, however, there was sand in his clothes, sand in his eyes, in his mouth and his nose, and sand in the open flesh on his back. Just when he thought he couldn't bear another minute, the wind died down, although it had slowed his pace greatly. He used the smallest amount of water possible to rinse his face and his mouth. Everything burned—his face, his feet, his back, his side—but he hiked on.

The sun set behind the clouds, and the temperature dropped off comfortably. The air was a bit humid and not quite as frigid as it had been on previous nights, which seemed a great luxury. At nearly ten that night, he began to see some far off lights in the distance. His spirits buoyed, he increased the pace of his stride.

Perhaps a mile from the town of Árido, a violent hissing sound was immediately followed by a razor-sharp pain just above his right ankle. He twisted around quickly and saw something scamper away quickly into the dark night—he thought it was a scorpion; he certainly couldn't tell if it was black or red. He moved on a few steps and then pulled up his pant leg to feel the bite—it was hot the touch.

By the time he reached Árido, his leg was almost completely numb. He dragged himself to the well just inside the gate and started to pump water into his mouth and then into his canteen. He poured some water on the sting and nearly shrieked in pain. Under the light of the street lamp, he could see that there was an inch-long piece of stinger still protruding from his leg. He put the strap of his canteen in his mouth and bit down on it, then with one swift pull yanked the stinger as hard as he could. Stars flashed before his eyes and the wound immediately pulsed blood. He pressed a used sock to it as hard as he could and sank down on his bottom. He wondered if he should try to find a doctor, but doubted there would even be one in a town this small—plus, the bandido said if it was red, he'd be dead, so it didn't much matter. So he waited. He sipped water and he waited.

"¿Quieres desayuno?"

"¿Qué?"

"You want breakfast?"

Santi had to force his eyes open through what felt like an inch of crust. He was still lying next to the well, a dreadfully skinny old woman looking down over him.

"Sixty centavos."

"For what?"

"For breakfast. Sixty centavos."

"Si, si, por favor."

He looked down at his injured leg. The sock was stuck to the wound. He peeled it back quickly and with a whimper. It didn't look nearly as bad as he thought it might. And he was still alive, so there was that.

He followed the old woman to her house, where he ate migas and drank tea. He asked if there was an inn and was told that she had a spare bed that would come with another breakfast for eighty centavos. With the knowledge of his frail condition and the prospects of another day in the desert and another act of penance ahead of him, Santi begrudgingly agreed. The woman's spare bed was a cot made of some sort of feathers stuffed in a burlap bag, but felt at that moment like the bed of a king. He fell asleep early that afternoon and did not wake until just before dawn. When he began to stir, the woman, whose name was Mina, prepared a breakfast identical to the previous day's. He washed and refilled at the well before setting out again.

That day was hotter than any previous and, though filled with soreness and pain, was otherwise uneventful. He arrived at Huerchito around eight that night. He paid forty centavos for a bowl of pollo soup with beans and some peppers before resentfully heading to the Shrine of Don Mentiroso, where he met Padre Pablo, who, after taking his donation, led him to the cellar where he was tied to a table by several townsmen. There was some prayer, some sacred oil, and then a thick cloth was placed over his face. The priest then poured water slowly over his mouth and nose. Santi coughed and gagged and struggled so fiercely against the restraints that he felt his arms and legs being held down by hand. The water and choking and suffocating continued until, just as he feared he might actually drown, the cloth and restraints were removed and he was allowed to vomit into a bucket beside the table. He was given his stamp and thanked for his donation before being tossed back out onto the road. His throat had never burned more.

He changed into dry clothes and dry boots and set out again. He began to think he would never survive this journey. Perhaps that was the point.

In three day's time, he reached the Church of Heavy Shoulders in Chalendo. He was, by this point, a shell of his former self. He shook constantly and coughed violently. It was here under Padre Aldo's care that he received his crown of thorns. Streams of blood ran down his face as he clenched his teeth in agony. He passed out in a field about a mile outside the city where his skin was picked at by mice during the night.

As the sun peaked over the mountain pass to the southeast, a soft hum first awakened his ears, then his mind—it was the sound of a motor. Seven or eight mice scurried off when he sat up and grabbed his belongings. He got to his knees just in time to see a brand-new Hispano-Suiza J12 thundering over the broad road and nearly straight in his direction. Santi rose to his feet to get a better view. The motor purred like a kitten—a stunningly beautiful car—all black, save the white wall tires. The luxury automobile slowed as it neared the pilgrim, then came to a complete stop. The driver waved Santi around to the passenger's side.

"I cannot ride, I am on the Pilgrimage of Sinners. I must walk."

"No, you idiota, somebody wants to talk to you."

Santi limped over to the passenger window and was shocked to see the paunchy face of Padre César.

"Well, pilgrim, how is your journey?"

"Horrible."

"It is meant to be a great trial—how, otherwise, would you curry a just god's favor?"

"How do you do it?"

"I," he began with a grotesque laugh. "I, do not have the soul of a padre who was an unconfessed sinner of the worst kind to deal with."

"At what point does god forgive? What must a man suffer?"

"He must suffer what is appointed to him to suffer."

"And what could a man have done—*any* man—to deserve such treatment as this?"

"Such treatment, you foolish idiota, such treatment is nothing compared with a soul lost to hellfire and torment for all eternity."

"What are mi padre's sins?"

"There are very serious sins."

"I'd like to know, that I may at least understand the weight of god's judgement on him, and me. Was my padre a thief?"

"Even worse."

"A killer?"

"Worse still."

"Worse?"

Padre César rocked back in his seat and then sprung forward, placing his chunky forearm on the door frame.

"He was the worst possible kind of sinner there can be."

Santi fell to his knees.

"There is no comfort for you on this journey, but in fulfilling it, you show mercy on the worst kind of man, and you break the curse on his future generations."

"I cannot do it. I have not the strength."

"Think of your niños, you selfish bastard. And do not deviate from the prescribed pilgrimage—not even a minute, not even a mile. One deviation and it's back to the beginning of the road—understand?"

Santi nodded his head.

"Now, since we had the fortuitous chance to meet here, while I am on the way to holiday by the sea, allow me to bless the rest of your journey, that god would bring you peace and show mercy on your sinner padre."

"I don't want your blessing."

"So be it. Drive on, driver."

And with that, the mammoth priest and the dazzling car were gone in a cloud of smoke and dust.

Santi's thoughts turned to Ana. She would understand if he did not make the additional voyage to Monterata, right? Simply put, the padre had forbidden it, and Santi was quite convinced he didn't have the strength to complete the journey if he disobeyed. He made up his mind—fifty or so miles on to Andachuo. Besides, he didn't believe in magic potions.

Trudging on in a southernly direction, Santi followed the prescribed path of pain. The first blisters he'd achieved had peeled and calloused and were replaced by an entirely new set. The weather began to feel more and more humid as he approached the mountain pass. The road curved sharply to the west and steeply downhill. Santi paused to look out over the terrain before him. He marveled at the sheer torture of it—miles of road sloping downward into a cavernous pit before a colossal hike straight up the side of a mountain. Both the descent and the climb were curses in their own right.

When he reached the lowest point on the road, he changed his socks and boots, ate some tortilla chips, and swabbed some salve he'd bought—and most likely overpaid—from an old cripple outside Chalendo, on his wounded forehead. He repacked his things and began to climb.

The path was indeed nearly straight up. He grabbed onto roots and limbs of various trees as he strained to scale the crag. Suddenly and without warning, black clouds rolled in over the peak and the temperature started dropping precipitously. A cold mist began to drizzle.

When Santi climbed to a point where the road leveled enough for him to stand straight up, he put his poncho over his head and wrapped himself in his warm coat.

The drizzle soon turned to rain, which almost immediately became sleet. He was thankful to come over a rim where the route arched off around the mountain rather than straight up it. The wind, however, howled here and snow even began to fall as he reached higher and higher elevations. His boots and socks were soaked through, his hands freezing, and his eyes raw from the gusting wind.

Just when Santi believed he'd been through the worst of it, he rounded a bend where the path was completely covered in snow. He would have begun to cry if he had the energy, but instead threw himself suicidally into the climb. He slipped and slid down, being blown off the course of the path with every attempt. He rushed the trail up the peak again, making more progress than he'd made on any previous attempt, until a gust of wind and a rush of falling snow sent him hurtling over the side of the path. Unable to control the pace or direction of his fall, he slid, rolled, and bounced through what thickets stood tall enough to reach through it. He landed with a thud, face down in the snow. He thought at that moment that while he would never see his precious Ana or his niños again, he would soon see his damned padre. He thought about all of the things he would tell him, all of the horrible names he would call him. He would curse him for being so selfish as to bring this horrible affliction upon him and his family. He would tell him he would never forgive, not even if it meant remaining in purgatory forever.

Santi slowly raised his head and almost, as if god himself had appeared, began to shudder with awe. Through a thin line of trees, between the flanks of two massive mountains, and under a harsh line of clouds, the sun was setting gloriously on the horizon. He closed his eyes and opened them again, this time nearly positive that he was seeing a mirage or having some kind of out of body experience. A rolling, lush valley sprawled in the direction of the sun, which appeared to be setting over water in the distance. He thought it might only be three or four miles—all downhill—to the path that opened up into the golden lowland. His choice was either to reach that valley or die on the side of that mountain. Certainly, he could not be blamed in this instance, for deviating off the course of the pilgrimage—his deviation, after all, had been unintentional. His mind resolved, he climbed to his feet and let the radiant valley draw his steps.

Over the course of a couple miles, the terrain leveled out—the snow morphed to freezing rain which became a pleasantly warm mist and then halted altogether. The path dried up until the only evidence of precipitation was the droplets of water dancing from leaf to leaf all around him. As he walked, the chirping of birds returned, and small creatures could be heard scurrying in the foliage underfoot. The air was warm enough that Santi removed his coat and poncho and paused to put dry socks and boots on. This path was even more rough than the pilgrimage—so much so that in places he could barely make it out. It was narrow and rugged and showed almost no evidence of use. At the foot of the mountain, the path curved for what felt like a mile around a thick grove of banyan trees and over the top of the ridge between the two mountains he'd seen from the elevated position of his fall. He gasped for air and energy as he ascended the incline. In the shadow of the two crags, it was nearly completely dark, but the moment he rose to the height of the ridge he was engulfed in radiance like he'd never before experienced. Everything, as far as his eyes could see was glowing and golden. The air was warm, and the breeze carried the hypnotic scent of summer wildflowers. He did his best to soak it all in, but the nagging thought did cross his mind that he might well be forced to start his death march all over again if he drifted too far into the valley. Down the path, however, an old wooden sign caught his eye. Something was written on it that he couldn't quite make out, but it intrigued him enough that he began walking in its direction.

He soon made out the distinctive shape of an arrow, pointing down the path, in the direction of the setting sun. On closer approach, Santi discerned the words: "Blessed Monasterio of the work of San Francisco de Monterata—five miles."

He couldn't believe his eyes. He was closer than he'd ever imagined he would be. He simply *had* to go now—didn't he? Could he tell his sweet Ana that he'd been within five miles of the magic potion she'd hoped would keep him alive and blessed of god, and not made the effort? At the same time, could he risk having all of the suffering he'd endured to this point negated? The sun was fading rapidly, so he decided to set up camp for the night and sleep on it. Santi noticed a small clearing to his left just beyond the path, under what looked to be a giant banana tree. The branches were so loaded with fruit that they nearly touched the ground. Santi helped himself greedily to five or six ripe bananas and made sure to pick many more to put in his sack. He started a small fire and set out his blanket. Before long he drifted to an exhausted, though slightly agitated slumber.

A crunching sound roused him from his uneasy sleep. His fire had died down but was still visible. He sat up slowly and looked around him. Approaching his position from the path was a dark figure, draped in a black robe. Santi grabbed for his knife and scrambled to his feet as the figure neared.

"Hello, there," a strong voice called.

"Who are you?"

"I saw your fire."

"And I saw you."

"Yes, of course you did."

"What do you want?"

"What do any of us want?"

"I don't know."

"Bananas."

"Bananas?"

"Yes, it is time for more bananas."

"Oh."

"Are you a pilgrim?" the hooded figure asked as it slowed to a halt just short of Santi's fire.

"Yes."

"I see."

"Are you?" Santi asked.

"Oh!" the figure laughed. "Yes, in a sense, I am."

"In a sense?"

"Yes. In a sense, I am a pilgrim just like you, on a very similar journey. In another sense, however, I am on a completely different journey—or at least in a very different place on that journey."

"I don't understand you."

"It's ok. You may later on."

"Later on?"

"On whose behalf do you walk the Pilgrimage of Sinners?"

"Mi padre."

"I see. He was a bad man?"

"That's what they tell me."

"And you did not know him very well?"

"Not at all. He abandoned me at the orphanage when I was six years old. I never saw him after that."

"And what was his sin that was unconfessed?"

"They will not tell me."

"I see," the figure mused. "It must have been a very serious sin then, no?"

"I would not be on this god-forsaken journey if it were not."

"God-forsaken? Why do you believe it is god-forsaken?"

"Because of what I have suffered."

"I think the path you walk is drenched in the presence of god."

"It is drenched in my suffering."

"Hear me, pilgrim, god is present in your suffering, though not in the way you might believe."

"I don't know. I'm beginning to wonder whether or not I actually believe in god at all."

"I see. Now that is a very serious sin."

"Is it?"

"One of the most serious—or at least that's what I'm told."

"Well, I'll make sure to confess and repent—if I ever make it home."

"Like a good hijo."

"I suppose."

"Do you mind if I pick some bananas?"

"Of course not."

The figure approached and began humming happily as he picked, placing the fruit gently in a sack slung over his shoulder.

"So you live around here?"

"Mhmm," came the content reply.

"In town?"

"Si."

"Is there anywhere there I can buy some food?"

"Why would you want to buy food?"

"Because I am hungry."

"Hungry?"

"Si."

"You're camping under a banana tree and you're hungry?"

"I was hoping to find something maybe more substantial than bananas."

"I see."

"So, is there somewhere?"

"Naturally."

"Ok."

"Did you know that you are off the path?"

"Si."

"They tell me a pilgrim who wanders off the Pilgrimage of Sinners must start from the beginning."

"I already have stamps."

"No matter. They'll know."

"How?"

"They have spies all over."

"Are you a spy?"

"Me?"

"Yes, you."

"That's a funny thought," the man said as he continued plucking bananas.

"So, *are* you?"

"I could be, and you wouldn't know it."

"Are you threatening me? I was blown off the path by a wicked snowstorm!"

"Calm yourself, calm yourself, pilgrim."

"Who are you?"

"My name?"

"Yes, your name."

"I am Padre Aránguiz."

"You are a *padre*?" Santi asked in horror.

"Si."

The pilgrim fell to his knees and began to whimper.

"Why do you cry?"

"You will force me to start over. I cannot do it—I do not have the strength."

The padre turned toward Santi, who was, for the first time, able to make out his face. He was middle-aged with a glorious black beard that looked like it had been oiled. His eyes were dark and gentle.

"I would not force you to start over."

"You would not?"

"Of course not—that would be barbaric."

"It would?"

"Si."

"It *would.*"

"Si. Stand—you need not kneel," he said kindly, offering his hand. "What is your name, pilgrim?"

"Santiago Vidal Perez."

"Santiago Vidal Perez?"

"Si."

"And what was your padre's name?"

"Iñigo Vidal Bustos."

The priest looked unconvincingly like he was trying to conceal a massive smile.

"Are you from the Blessed Monasterio of the work of—".

"San Francisco de Monterata? Si."

Santi chuckled to himself while taking the padre's hand.

"What's so funny?"

"Mi esposa, she begged me to find the monasterio and drink from the magic potion."

"The magic potion?"

"Si. She thinks it will bless me and cure my ills. She even sent me with a chalice."

"Your esposa is a smart mujer, with much faith."

"She is."

"And you—do you not hold the same faith?"

"I don't know. I suppose I was raised to believe, but this journey has made it much harder."

"Because of your suffering?"

"Because of what is demanded. The elements, the blisters, the walking, I can deal with. It is the cruelty that has turned my heart against god."

"Has god been cruel to you?"

"Very."

"I see," the padre nodded solemnly.

The two men stood in silent communion with the rising sun.

"Would you like to drink of the potion?"

"I'm not sure."

"It may heal your ills, as your esposa believes."

"But I will have to start the pilgrimage all over."

"One thing I can promise you—it will be your decision."

"I don't understand."

"If you come and talk with me, and drink the potion, you will have a choice—to start over or not at all."

"But mi padre's soul—"

"The choice will be yours."

"Mi niños—"

"Come with me, pilgrim. I promise I will lighten your load—*if* you will allow it."

"I cannot leave the path."

"Your choice this very day is between staying on the path and losing your faith, or stepping out into the unknown—the mystical, the mysterious—and, perhaps, saving your soul."

"But the church says that I will certainly—"

"Certainty is not faith. Certainty is idolatry, mi hijo. If you truly seek god and his mercy, you will not find it on that path. You will only find it in walking away, and that is a true act of faith."

Santi looked uneasily over his shoulder toward the mountain pass, then back toward the padre.

"If you seek the mercy of god, walk with me. I will not fail to lighten your load, pilgrim."

Santi stood and gathered his belongings. The padre smiled broadly.

"Let me have your stamp book."

Santi handed it to the priest with a momentary hesitation. Padre Aránguiz tossed it in the fire. The pilgrim nearly dove in after it instinctively. Those stamps represented so much work, so much pain, and so many scars.

"You're free to start over," the priest said. "But I doubt you'll want to."

Santi's pained gaze turned to resignation.

"Come."

The two men walked side by side down the narrow road—the padre and the pilgrim.

As the day brightened, Santi was able to make out for the first time that the better part of the valley was actually a well-cultivated vineyard, with rows of herbs, medicinal plants, and exotic flowers scattered in. The fragrance was marvelous. After walking a mile or two in silence, taking in the enchanting surroundings and strange sense of peace this padre seemed to emanate, the monasterio came into view—a mission-style church, painted white, surrounded by countless rose bushes. Past the monasterio and the small village sprawled the mighty sea.

"What makes you think the souls of your niños are in peril?" Padre Aránguiz suddenly asked.

"The padre in my hometown says so."

"Do you beat your children?"

"What?"

"Do you beat your children?"

"Of course not, I love them dearly."

"Would you ever put any one of your children through what you have endured to this point?"

"Of course not."

"Not even if they had sinned greatly against you?"

"Of course not. I would not wish this on my worst enemy."

"Because you are a *good* padre, no?"

"Si."

"And you *love* your niños, no?"

"Si, with all of my heart."

"Who told you that you must undertake such a pilgrimage?"

"Padre César, the padre at the church in my town."

"I see. And who beat you before you left?"

"The townspeople."

"I see. And who put you in the pillory and whipped you and robbed you of your human dignity in Concurra?"

"You know about that?"

"Si."

"It was Padre Miguel."

"And who threw rotten food at you and tore at your hair while you were incapacitated there?"

"The people of Concurra."

"I see. And who tortured you in the dungeon in Huerchito?"

"Padre Pablo."

"I see. And who scarred your head with a crown of thorns in Chalendo?"

"Padre Aldo."

"I see."

The two men then walked on silently until they reached the open gate of the monasterio. Santi stopped.

"Well, will you come in?" asked Padre Aránguiz.

"But I am a sinner. It is a holy place."

"Do not allow superstition to halt your journey, now. *Everyone* is welcome here," the padre said kindly, putting a hand on the pilgrim's shoulder.

Santi looked about nervously.

"And the magic potion?"

"We will get to that," the priest said with a laugh. "But first, you must eat."

Inside an open hall, Santi was seated at an enormous table along-side several monks and friars who welcomed him warmly. He became self-conscious of his surely worn appearance and most definitely offensive smell, but they did not seem to notice. There was coffee served with huevos, peppers, beans, freshly baked tortillas, and fried bananas—naturally—alongside a merry dose of laughter. It was pure, almost childlike laughter. It reminded Santi of the way his niños laughed when he tickled them or kissed the underside of their necks. The monks kept serving him, plateful after plateful of delicious, hot food, until he was so full, he thought he might burst.

After the meal, he was shown to a room where he was given new clothes and shoes and was allowed to bathe. He sat in the warm water, sure that he would be rushed out soon, but he never was. Once he was clean and relaxed, he dressed and peeked out into the long hallway. He started down toward the echoing sound of chanting until he reached what must have been the main chapel. It was a large, round room, full of windows and light. There were priests and monks and friars and even laypeople, arranged in a large circle, singing and chanting together. There was heartfelt reverence in their prayers—not contrived or obligatory like Santi was used to feeling in church, but natural and pure in much the same way their laughter had been at breakfast.

There was something truly mystical about the place—he thought it must have something to do with the magic potion. There was lightness and significance there. Levity and reverence. Reality and hope. All in equal measure and all without fear.

Santi simply stood and watched the service. When it was finished, Padre Aránguiz rose and greeted him with a warm hug.

"Let's go talk," the priest said, taking Santi by the hands.

They walked through the back of the nearly indistinguishable chancel and out into the warm, fragrant air. There was a well-worn path that led through the vineyard toward another white building on the hill overlooking the mighty sea.

"How do you feel now that you've eaten and bathed?"

"Human," Santi replied.

"Wonderful."

Holy men and ordinary men alike passed them in both directions as they strolled the path.

"How are the shoes?"

"They need to be broken in," the pilgrim answered with a chuckle.

The priest laughed heartily.

"Santi, you told me about your journey, about all the things you endured."

"Si."

"But you never told me when you were treated cruelly by god."

"Has the entire journey not been required by him?"

"You told me it was Padre César that required it of you."

"Does he not speak for god?"

"Does he?"

Santi shrugged.

"It was not god who locked you in the pillory and took flesh from your back—it was a man. It was not god who tortured you in a dark dungeon—it was a man. It was not god who thrust a crown of thorns upon your brow—it was a man. It was not god who was cruel to you, it was men."

They reached the beautifully unassuming building at the top of the ridge. A warm, salty breeze blew through their hair. There was a tap on the wall that stuck out over an empty fountain. A sign on the wall read, "For the Fortification of Pilgrims."

"You believe that god is a good padre, no?"

"Si—I think so."

"If he is indeed a good padre, like you are a good padre, how can it be that he requires such barbarity? And for what—to earn his favor?"

"It is justice. If he was not just—"

"Retribution is far different than justice. Santi, as you would not mistreat your niños, neither does god mistreat you."

Santi's frail body racked with sobs.

"But the pilgrimage—"

"This is the great truth that may set your soul at ease—god does not require violence and bloodshed in exchange for forgiveness—men do."

Tears streamed down the pilgrims cheeks.

"God is not like us. His justice does not demand barbarity—it does not destroy, it *restores*. Men may be violent, but he is not."

"I've never heard such a thing," the pilgrim said through his sobs.

"Do you know that your padre lived here the last twenty-five years of his life?"

"You knew mi padre?"

"Si, he was also under my care."

"How is this so?"

"He was forced to leave you and your town by Padre César—forced to walk the Pilgrimage of Sinners at the barrel of a gun because he refused to believe in a god who lusted after blood."

"But he left me—"

"He had no choice, Santi. After he found his way here, much the same way you did, he took some time to heal and then tried to get you back many times, but the church would not allow it. You must know that it was never his will to leave you. Would you like to know what sins he was accused of that were so serious as to separate him from the niño he loved so dearly?"

Santi simply nodded.

"He was labeled a drunkard and a heretic. He was a drunkard because he drank wine without completing the Pilgrimage of Sinners, and a heretic because he believed in a god whose nature was love and mercy, not death and cruelty."

The pilgrim could no longer hold back his emotions. He sank to his knees and wept.

"Now, pilgrim, you may fill your chalice."

Santi rose slowly and extended the chalice. When he pulled the handle, a blood-red liquid flowed from its polished stainless-steel tap.

"Fill your cup," Padre Aránguiz said. "Fill it up."

When the chalice was filled, Santi drew it to his face and smelled.

"This is wine," he said in astonishment.

"Si."

"But it is not magic? It is not a sacred potion?"

"Is it not sacred? The monks here have been making this wine for nearly five-hundred years and giving it away every day to fortify weary pilgrims like you and me."

"I will certainly be disqualified."

"You may be disqualified by men, dear pilgrim, but you will never be disqualified by god."

Santi's face contorted as he stammered, "And do you require a donation for the wine?"

"Of course not," Padre Aránguiz replied. "It is as god's forgiveness—*freely given*."

The pilgrim sipped the wine through his sobs and then began to convulse. He collapsed to the ground, drinking the sweet, ruby colored nectar. Padre Aránguiz knelt beside him, taking the shaking pilgrim in his arms.

"This is what god has done for you. This is why there is wine—it is all a gift, it is all sacred, and it is all for *you*, pilgrim."

Santi imbibed fervently, brimming with peace and hope.

"Drink, dear Santi, *and be loved by god*."

Three nights later, Santi's family was whisked away by truck in the dark of night by monks from the Blessed Monasterio of the work of San Francisco de Monterata. Ana gave birth a week later to a boy who was christened Iñigo. The family were settled in a white house on the outskirts of the merciful town of Monterata, overlooking the majestic blue sea, where Santi learned to grow grapes for wine and began building motors again.

Written in the book in Padre César's room, next to the name Santiago Vidal Perez, were the words:

*Drunkard, Heretic.*

**Fin.**

# OPEN HANDS

D on't deconstruct.
There. I said it.

Don't do it.

Or, if you do, only deconstruct to the extent that you reach predetermined answers.

*Our* answers.

Remember, we're supposed to hold fast to the profession of our faith.

If you start doubting one area, what's to say you won't doubt the rest?

After all, there can only be one truth.

And you should consider yourself lucky—*blessed*, I should say—that out of the thousands of different religions on the planet, and the tens of thousands of Christian denominations alone, you stumbled upon the right one.

Oh, and make sure you put your love gift in the basket as it goes by … you know, above and beyond your weekly tithe, because the parsonage needs a new jacuzzi tub in the master.

## CREED

It would almost be comical if it wasn't so harmful, right? If people weren't actually being abused at the hands of a system designed to keep us all in line.

But first, let me get this out in the open: I'm still a confessing Christian.

I affirm the Apostles' Creed. And I don't do it because I'm convinced of its truth in an intellectual way. I affirm it because I chose to. It connects me with a beautiful faith tradition and I like that.

I affirm the Apostles' Creed because I hold it in open hands, rather than clenched fists.

I first came across that concept in a truly astounding little book called *Bring Prayer into Your Life With Open Hands* by Henri Nouwen, and it's become something of a Rosetta Stone by which I view the world.

So I say that I hold it in open hands because I might be wrong.

And I'm fine with that.

## TURTLES & TABERNACLES

Another step backward, so you'll know a little about where I'm coming from.

I was raised in northeastern New Jersey—not exactly a hotbed of church culture, but I came from a family where faith was important.

You see, my grandparents on my mom's side were born in the Soviet Union and only escaped after being displaced by the Second World War. They came to the states with the knowledge that their Christian brothers and sisters left behind were suffering unimaginable evils because of their faith.

So being born in America, where you could practice your faith freely and openly, was a privilege not to be taken lightly. Taking a serious faith seriously was a responsibility you owed to those believers huddled in secret meetings, those brave brothers and sisters clinging to their faith in a Gulag, and those martyrs who had already lost their lives for the sake of Jesus.

I'd say that's pretty heavy for a five year old, but I was all about it.

In fact, I remember praying within earshot of an adult relative one day—I want to say I was still in kindergarten—and thanking God that he "*could even love scum like me.*"

The only reason I remember this particular prayer is that after I was done, this person said, "Maybe if you pray in front of people—like in Sunday school or something—don't say 'scum.' Say 'sinner' instead."

*Think about that.*

The level of indoctrination.

And I don't just mean me … I mean, check out the level that my relatives had been force-fed the Kool-aid.

He was not correcting my theology—the belief that I, the Ninja Turtle obsessed, sensitive kid with the sandy blonde baby curls, was *scum in God's eyes.*

What he was correcting, was *how to display that faith for the approval of others.*

And man, what a damaging, soul-smothering message that was.

(Caveat here: my family is amazing. We have all been on our own journeys but have still journeyed together.)

But at that point in my life, I literally believed that you could "lose your salvation" at the drop of a hat. Much groveling was required to stay in God's good graces.

And ongoing groveling, too.

As in, if I died in my sleep, having *one sin* that remained uncon-fessed, I would spend eternity burning in a hell-fire that no stop, drop, and roll the fireman at school taught us could save me from.

And this all stemmed from this idea that God is so holy and human beings are so inherently flawed and evil, that we should be thrilled with anything better than eternity in hell ... Including a life of self-immolation and salvation anxiety.

Speaking of kindergarten (and those blessed, pizza-eating mutants), I brought a Ninja Turtles crayon box in to my conservative Christian private school. Maybe the second day of school, my teacher went on a rant about neither she—nor the stern, oft-red-faced and yelling principal—liked the Ninja Turtles, because *God didn't like stories about mutants or ninjas.*

I spent the entire school year with that box face down on my desk so that she would not catch a glimpse of the evil, half-shelled objects of God's wrath.

And the thing is, I wasn't really worried about getting in "trouble" about it ...

*I was worried that she would think less of me.*

My next early church memory was listening to a very, very special guest who came to speak in my third grade Sunday school class.

This guest was to be revered, honored, and even imitated.

This person was *a missionary.*

And not any old missionary.

This person was a missionary *in Africa.*

And this missionary told us about how awful things were in Africa—starvation and disease and backwards tribal bush people who worship the devil and are possessed by demons—and how the only hope for these poor, sorry Africans was Jesus.

(*Side note: RACIST MUCH!?*)

That's why this missionary needed our money—*they literally asked eight year olds for money*—so that this missionary could tell more Africans about Jesus.

I remember another kid raising his hand and asking why we didn't just feed the starving children, since they were … you know … starving.

And because, you know, that *actually seemed to be the problem* …

This missionary's answer was burned into my mind and was perhaps the earliest step in my deconstruction: "*Well, we don't have enough to feed everyone, but we* can *tell everyone about Jesus, and that way,* they can at least go to heaven."

Ten year old me thought: something doesn't sound right about that.

Thirty-six year old me will reinterpret for you: *that's some steaming horse shit right there.*

A couple years later, I was struck by the thought that other people had other religions, and that those others religions taught that if I didn't believe in that religion, I would end up in hell.

So I asked my grandfather one day: "Papa, how do we know that the God we believe in is the right God?"

His response?

"That's the devil in your mind. Don't ask that question or he'll get a foothold."

*Hold that faith with closed fists, young'un.*

I remember even then being massively dissatisfied with that answer, but I tried to take it in stride.

(Another side note: my grandfather was, is, and always will be one of my absolute heroes. He will always remain one of the best people, and yes, one of the truest, most merciful Christians, I've ever known.)

Then in high school, my family had a major falling out with the only church I'd ever called home, and things got weird.

I started having all sorts of doubts that my clenched knuckles strained against. I specifically remember waking up one morning and thinking—I believe in spiritual warfare? Angels and demons and all sorts of spirits flying around my head that I cannot see or detect, other than maybe some vague creepy feeling if I'm lucky? Sounds like a fairy tale.

But of course, you have to *hold on* to your faith. So I did my best.

For a period of time, my family ended up driving to Brooklyn every Sunday morning (and many Tuesday nights) to attend a massive, Pentecostal, speak-in-tongues kind of church. Let me say here that this was not what we were used to, but there was something undeniably alive and healing in that place, and we needed that.

It was in that tabernacle that I opened myself up to the idea that God really does move among us and through us. I started "feeling" God all over the place, and that became almost like a drug.

And this place had like, advertised miracles happening. As in, they put out DVDs about people in their church who had been instantaneously and miraculously healed from disease, abuse, and decades of drug addiction.

The funny thing was … that kind of thing never seemed to happen around *me*.

I was taught, just *pray more* if you want to see God work like that. So I did.

Still nothing? *Read the Bible more.*

So I did.

Still nothing? *Worship more.*

And I did.

Still nothing.

The relationships around me were still broken.

Friends were were still battling addiction.

And I was still convinced that I was scum in God's eyes, because otherwise, he would show up …

*Wouldn't he?*

My knuckles were turning red.

*Just hold on, Brandon. Hold on to it.*

Then, I was introduced to C.S. Lewis my senior year at the super-conservative Christian high school I attended. And that allowed me to breathe and relax my grip a little. See, I learned from C.S. Lewis that you didn't have to sacrifice your intellectual integrity to have belief in God. That's a great lesson.

What followed, however ... not so much.

You see, that led me down the rabbit hole of apologetics.

I read books about how God could be proved to exist, and how if I still had doubts, I should remember the book of Job: *who was I to question God?*

(Remember, I was still scum!)

I was taught to be ready to give an answer that would defend the faith (my Christian high school's "mascot" was a "Defender"—a cartoon dressed up in Roman garb who was supposed to spur us on to victory not only on the basketball court, but in the courts of our hearts. Or something like that ... didn't make much sense then either...).

*Again—closed fists.*

I even started reading books by prominent atheists simply in order to criticize their arguments in the margins with all the knowledge I'd amassed about how wrong they were.

I thought I'd arrived.

I understood it all.

It all made sense.

Until it didn't.

# CRACKS

From there, it was off to Nashville to pursue my dream of being a singer-songwriter in the mold of John Mayer because after all, it was 2003. I pursued that dream for a while, and might have actually been mediocre, but then life swooped in. I married my college sweetheart and started working real jobs. I wanted a stable life, kids, cats, and I don't know, *something more*. I still thought about maybe being a worship leader, or even "planting" my own church, but that was also a lot of work.

My wife and I tried church after church in and around Nashville, and just didn't feel like we belonged anywhere.

In one place, the pastor mocked the recently released movie, *The DaVinci Code*, devoting an entire forty minute message to repeating things like, "How dare they question the Wurrrd of Gaaaawd!" These proclamations were met with thunderous applause, by the way.

In another place, the preacher devoted an entire message to mocking fat people. I'm literally not kidding. He tried using the part of the Bible where it says Samuel was impressed by David's appearance (gay Freudian slip anyone?) to tell us that it was a sin not to be lean and muscled.

On yet another stop, a man who knew we were visiting approached me during the alter call and told me he had a word from God specifically for me. I was so excited—so ready for God to finally show up and speak into my life in a supernatural way. The man put his hand on my head and made several very bold statements about my life—you're a student athlete, you attend such and such university, etc.—*all of which were wrong.*

Which led me wonder ... are we just making all of this up as we go?

Then I started reading Rob Bell.

You probably haven't heard of him.

(That's sarcasm).

And I remember thinking, "Eww, this is uncomfortable ... If we start doubting *these* beliefs, where do we stop? We can't just doubt *all of them* ... right?"

Then the thought struck me: *why not?*

I mean, if it's true, it'll withstand honest doubt ... right?

My grip loosened ever so slightly.

# ONE LAST SQUEEZE

Then, I decided to jump in deep one last time—to let God prove himself to me once and for all. I took a job in ministry with a very conservative organization doing fantastic work and making a difference in the lives of very vulnerable people.

I thought this was it—I thought God had taken me on this long road to lead me to this particular place where I would finally find my niche, finally see my miracles, and finally experience fullness, peace, and a life of faith that would come as second nature.

Only, I had to raise my own support (meaning, my own salary).

That's okay! I'm was going to jump in!

I was prayed over and counseled by more spiritual mentors than I can remember that I would never be in God's debt—*he would always show up* just when I needed him the most.

When our mortgage was due and we lacked seven hundred thirty six dollars and twenty nine cents to make the payment, I could expect a check to miraculously show up in the mail for seven hundred thirty six dollars and twenty nine cents!

*This was going to be amazing!*

Well, six months and twelve thousands dollars of credit card and medical debt later, it certainly seemed that the post was running awfully slow.

And when I brought this up to those same people who had told me to trust the promises of God, suddenly, the situation seemed to be conspicuously *my fault.*

*How is your prayer life?*

*Did you pray over those particular support letters individually?*

*Do you have unconfessed sin issues?*

So here we are again—God doesn't show up in my life like he does in other people's lives.

Why?

Because you're scum, Brandon.

As Nashville Predators fans charmingly chant to opposing goalies after scoring against them:

"You suck. It's all your fault. It's all your fault."

You're the reason there's no power.

You're the reason there's no money.

You're the reason the church is flailing.

*You're the bad one, Brandon.*


# EMPTY HANDED

After that experience I found myself broken, depressed, and spiritually numb. I was really angry at God because I knew I'd done everything right—I'd followed the plan.

He was the one who hadn't bothered to do his part.

It was around this time that "Love Wins" came out—you know, that horrible, dangerous book by that earlier mentioned man to whom we've since bid farewell.

And I was on board.

But get this …

I came to the belief that God was so good, so loving, and so forgiving that he would literally forgive every single person who ever lived … And yet, he still didn't like *me*.

That Christmas, kind of on a whim, my wife bought me *Beauty Will Save the World* by Brian Zahnd. I started reading it few weeks later and I could not, for the life of me, figure it out.

What was this guy saying?

Was he some sort of liberal charlatan?

He kept talking about violence and the Sermon on the Mount and how Evangelicalism was too closely aligned with American political agendas …

I literally had no clue how to wrap my mind around it—and he was using language I'd heard in church for thirty years.

So I did what anyone would do—I looked him up on YouTube.

I watched an older message of his called *A Beautiful Gospel*, and in this message, he talks about how if Jesus is God, Jesus would show us what God is like. Brian would say, "God is like Jesus. God has always been like Jesus. We haven't always known this, but now we do."

So when the woman caught in adultery is brought before Jesus, and the religious people challenge him on what to do—you know, *because the Bible says we should stone her*—Jesus sends them away, telling her that he does not condemn her.

As Brian noted, we don't ever see Jesus turning people away because of their flaws, because of their humanness. He ate with the "sinners," got drunk with them, hung out with prostitutes, and healed the hearts of those wrestling with demons.

In fact, the only people who turned human beings away in the gospel narratives were the Pharisees.

And that was the biggest moment in my "re-construction"—it dawned on me that *I had been chasing after the approval of a cosmic Pharisee my entire life.*

Because the Pharisees condemned her to death, but *God* did not condemn at all.

And she didn't have to do a thing.

She didn't have to clean up her act.

She didn't have to grovel for forgiveness.

*God hadn't condemned her in the first place.*

I realized at that moment that if God was real, he must be like Jesus, and that Jesus was someone who would like me—he'd want to grab a beer with me at Fleet Street Pub and watch Arsenal, God's chosen football club.

*Because I wasn't scum to the God who looks like Jesus.*

And I didn't have to earn her favor.

*I'd never lost it.*

It was during this message that, for the first time in my life, I opened my fists.

And saw that *my hands were empty.*

There was nothing there.

All this time, I had been clutching air.

I slowly began to understand that with open hands, palms up, I could actually receive something, enjoy humanity, and simply be loved.

I could have stayed on the path, clutching at ozone, but I would have lost my faith.

Instead, I opened my fists and walked away.

And it saved my soul.

# REPENTANCE

So where did that land me?

It's led me to a holistic faith that I hold with open hands, rather than clenched fists.

Because *(shrugs shoulders)* I could be wrong.

But I do believe that if there is a God, he looks like Jesus.

And I believe that our understanding of God is stilted if it's boiled down to a legal transaction, a question of "if you died tonight..."

So no more bronze aged child sacrifice.

No more condemnation of people with different beliefs or no beliefs at all.

No more Bible verse karate to prove how right I am.

No more believing that my daughters (or anyone else) are inherently depraved.

No more thinking that one political party is good and the other is evil.

No more bitterness for where other people are on their journey.

No more pressure to conform.

*No more believing that I'm scum.*

And God, it feels great.

I have never been so free in my life.

Free to reconsider points of view when I'm presented with new information.

Free to love people without coercing them to a particular way of thinking.

Free to teach my daughters that God will always love them no matter what, that their dad will always love them no matter what, and that kindness is magic.

Free to advocate for people who have done horrible things.

Free to believe that which resonates with my soul without trying to possess it.

Free to see the good in people, even when they hurt me.

Free to rest and create and risk and hope.

And most satisfyingly, I'm free to call bullshit when I see it.

So if any part of my journey sounds familiar, I'd say keep going.

Clear out all the mental furniture and burn some sage in the room of your mind.

Be angry because you were let down by the cosmic Pharisee and others.

It's okay, she can handle it.

So rage, cry, and shake your fists.

Then open up them and receive whatever it is that comes to you.

It may look completely different than my experience, but I'd be willing to bet it's better than where you've been. That's not to say it will be easy, but you will be free to accept whatever gifts life offers with open hands.

# ISOLATED AND UNHEARD

## CAN RESTORATIVE JUSTICE PRACTICES OFFER BETTER OUTCOMES FOR BOTH OFFENDERS AND VICTIMS OF CRIME THAN CURRENT RETRIBUTIVE SENTENCING POLICY?

{ SENTENCING LAW, FALL 2021}

## INTRODUCTION

"I t won't bring my son back."

This oft-echoed sentiment in courtroom dramas on television and in movies encapsulates the pain, grief, and longing for justice felt by victims of violent crime. The phrase drives at the heart of the very human understanding of the shortcomings inherent in any criminal justice system—mainly that some wrongful act has taken place that cannot be undone. For the person who utters this phrase or one like it, the sentiment is that the person responsible should have the worst done to them that the law allows—and perhaps even more, because even the worst is not enough to rectify the harm done.

The maddening reality is that no amount of suffering or punishment endured by an offender could ever bring a murdered loved one back from the dead or heal the physical and psychological scars that victims of crime are left to live with. In a case as extreme as murder, the victim's loved ones are still left to grieve alone, even after a life sentence is declared or an execution is carried out. However, victims of even non-violent crimes are often left feeling ignored or even abused by the current criminal justice system, as the state's interests in meting out punishment can be directly at odds with a victim's interests in being made whole.[1]

At the same time, under the looming threat of incarceration, criminal defendants are usually advised by their attorneys—and wisely so—to refrain from even speaking about the charges against them. Even the act of pleading guilty to a lesser charge in exchange for a lesser degree of punishment is, perhaps paradoxically, an avoidance of full acceptance of responsibility for the extent of the harms committed, and often leaves victims with the lingering sense of bitterness that justice was left undone.[2]

Undoubtedly, there are some offenders for which incapacitation is the only way to ensure the safety of the population at large.[3] Further, the punishment and deterrence of crime are certainly far from ignoble aims in a civilized society. But if pure incapacitation and punishment by incarceration are the accomplished goals of the criminal justice system, victims of crime remain saddled with the consequences of a wrongdoer's actions, and the wrongdoers remain incentivized to avoid responsibility for their actions.[4]

And victims of crime are not the only ones being failed by the current retributive sentencing schemes. The rate at which the American criminal justice system feeds citizens into prisons is the highest in the world.[5] Compounding the sheer number of people incarcerated are the lingering effects suffered by offenders in stigmatization, collateral consequences, and isolation from their own communities.[6] The barriers erected in an offender's path after they have supposedly completed their term of punishment only exacerbates the very real experience of alienation from society.[7] The fact that retributive sentencing policies fail to provide a walkable path toward reintegration back into community life is a major contributor to the extraordinarily high rates of recidivism in the United States.[8]

Restorative justice, by contrast, is a sentencing philosophy that incorporates a diverse and evolving set of practices, and offers a different blueprint for thinking about both justice and victims' rights.[9] This philosophy understands justice not simply as punishment or retribution, but as an ideal where the harms caused and the relationships destroyed by crime are repaired to the fullest extent possible.[10] While there is no authoritative definition of restorative justice, proponents maintain a shared belief in the importance of meeting the needs of victims, accountability for the offender, and participation by the interested parties in repairing the harm to some extent while promoting reintegration into the community.[11] Restorative justice philosophy understands crime as harm done to individuals and communities which results in obligations, and invites those affected to engage in the process of justice.[12] Additionally, restorative justice philosophy recognizes that "punishment alone is unlikely to convince the offender to become a contributing member of society," and therefore recognizes the need for accountability which reaches deeper than an offender sitting in a prison cell.[13] At its core, it aims to allow victims of crime to make key decisions in the process, make the justice system more therapeutic for all parties, and thereby reduce the likelihood of enduring trauma and recidivism.[14]

So, rather than focusing solely on prosecuting guilt and punishment from the purely macro, traditional "State vs. Offender" perspective, restorative justice practices provide the opportunity for both individual healing and lasting societal change.[15] This sentencing philosophy seeks to address the interconnection between both the causes and consequences of crime.[16] By focusing on the harm caused, rather than simply the punishment deserved, restorative justice practices aim "to provide an experience of healing for all concerned."[17]

In practice, restorative justice is a process by which wrongdoers, victims of crime, and their surrounding communities are brought together "to address the harm inflicted by a crime and agree upon a series of measures designed to repair that harm rather than meting out punishment."[18] By bringing the relevant sides to the table together, restorative justice schemes have the potential to reduce prison populations and recidivism by helping to bridge the divide between offender and victim and establishing a pathway back into the community for both.[19] These types of programs accomplish this by fostering the type of dialogue that allows for acceptance of responsibility by the wrongdoer while offering more satisfaction and closure to the injured party.[20] This is achieved first by allowing victims to be heard by offenders, offering the opportunity for offenders to understand the consequences of their actions on a more human and personalized level.[21] At the same time, providing a mechanism for victims to learn firsthand about offenders can foster empathy and transform feelings of victimhood into a more positive psychological state of being.[22]

This paper will first examine the current state of sentencing in the criminal justice system, including rates of incarceration and recidivism. Next, the disconnect between the adversarial criminal justice process and victims of crime, offenders, and their communities will be explored with an eye toward areas in which restorative justice practices could achieve understanding and even reconciliation. Finally, this paper will examine how restorative justice practices could better meet the needs of parties affected by crime, and how those practices may allow for the reduction of incarceration while fostering the reintegration of both victims and offenders into the community.

# PART I: RETRIBUTIVE SENTENCING PHILOSOPHY'S OUTCOME: MASS INCARCERATION AND RECIDIVISM

In order to understand the effects of retributive sentencing policies on offenders, victims, and whole communities, it is necessary to consider the system as it currently exists. This section will discuss how, in an effort to curtail high crime rates, the implementation of retributive sentencing schemes has created a globally unparalleled system of mass incarceration and how that system feeds directly into high rates of recidivism.

## a. Mass Incarceration and Crime Rates

The term "mass incarceration" has grown into something of a cliché, though it certainly has the ring of truth, given the current state of the prison system in the United States. While only possessing five percent of the population of the world, the United States is home to twenty percent of the world's prisoners.[23] Nearly one out of every one hundred adults in the United States is currently incarcerated.[24] Political rallying cries such as getting "tough on crime," "the war on drugs," and "three-strikes-and-you're out" laws, birthed out of the noble desire of reducing soaring violent crime and drug addiction rates from the 1960s through the 1990s, have served to drastically drive incarceration rates upward.[25] As a result, the country's imprisoned population surged nearly five hundred percent in the years between 1974 and 2007.[26] The United States currently boasts higher per capita incarceration rates than countries like Iran, Zimbabwe, "and even notoriously punitive Singapore."[27] By the early twentieth century, the trend toward mass incarceration earned the United States the moniker of "the most punitive democracy in the world."[28]

Considering the precipitous decline in crime rates the nation experienced over the last several decades, it would be tempting to credit the policies which led to mass incarceration with achieving its desired effect.[29] After all, the 1991 peak crime rate fell nearly in half by 2017, and property crimes have reached their lowest levels since 1967.[30] It is inviting to draw a correlation between the sixty-one percent increase in imprisonment between 1990 and 2013 and the fifty-percent decline in violent crime achieved during that same period.[31] The counter-intuitive truth, however, is that social and economic factors, such as wage growth and the aging population, have been determined by social science research to be the main drivers of the drastic plummet of nationwide crime rates.[32]

To that effect, divergences in state incarceration policies demonstrate that sheer incarceration itself does not correlate directly with lower crime rates. Louisiana, for example, boasted a 2013 rate of incarceration higher than anywhere else in the world, imprisoning one out of seventy-five adults.[33] However, despite leading the nation—and the globe for that matter—in incarceration rates, the state failed over time to achieve any appreciable decline in crime when compared to the national average.[34] Pennsylvania, on the other hand, boasts a crime rate twenty-two percent lower than the national average while incarcerating its citizens at a drastically lower rate than Louisiana.[35] Likewise, in the years between 1992 and 2012, New Jersey, New York, Texas, and California all saw drastic decreases in crime rates when compared to the national average, while at the same time cutting prison populations by more than twenty percent.[36] Ultimately, it seems that the retributive sentencing policies which led to the current state of mass incarceration were birthed out of a "knee-jerk reaction to crime," while lacking foundation in scientific or sociological rationale.[37]

## b. Mass Incarceration and Recidivism Rates

Exacerbating the crisis of mass incarceration is the issue of recidivism and the substantial likelihood that a person who has been incarcerated will end up behind bars again. Recidivism is defined by the United States Sentencing Commission as "a person's relapse into criminal behavior, often after the person receives sanctions or undergoes intervention for a previous crime."[38] According to the United States Bureau of Justice Statistics in 2012, nearly two thirds of those prisoners released annually will recidivate within three years.[39]

While, for a number of reasons, there does not appear to be a definitive consensus on the effects of incarceration on recidivism, as data continues to emerge, some studies show that imprisonment "can actually lead people to commit more crimes after release."[40] Research has additionally demonstrated that the more punitive and restrictive the incarceration regime, the more likely an offender is to recidivate upon release.[41] In 2020, on the other hand, the United States Sentencing Commission reported that offenders incarcerated for one hundred-twenty months or more were approximately thirty percent less likely to recidivate than those serving shorter sentences.[42] There are undoubtedly a multitude of factors that might cause an offender serving a longer sentence not to recidivate–such as age at time of release and the effect of a long sentence in sheer deterrence–but the fact remains that the United States maintains not only the highest rates of incarceration in the world, but one of the highest criminal recidivism rates as well.[43]

## PART II: RETRIBUTIVE SENTENCING POLICY AND ITS EFFECTS ON OFFENDERS, COMMUNITIES, AND VICTIMS

If it is not clear that retributive sentences deter further criminal behavior, there is still an underlying argument that crime deserves punishment meted out by the government.[44] While this certainly may be true to some degree, a sentencing philosophy that focuses almost exclusively on retribution fails to consider the long-term effects of that punishment. This section discusses the effects of retributive sentencing within the adversarial criminal justice system on offenders, victims, and their communities.

## a. The Effects of Retributive Incarceration on Offenders

### 1. OFFENDERS HAVE INCENTIVES TO AVOID RESPONSIBILITY

In its landmark decision *Miranda v. Arizona*, the United States Supreme Court held that a person in custodial interrogation must be given a warning that most Americans can now recite, albeit imprecisely: "you have the right to remain silent; anything you say can and will be used against you in a court of law."[45] While the exact language of the warning is not required,[46] the purpose of putting a criminal suspect on notice that he cannot be compelled to be a witness against himself is rooted in the Court's understanding that an individual's Fifth Amendment right against self-incrimination is "fundamental to our system of constitutional rule."[47] In a later concurring opinion by Justice O'Connor, joined by Justice Scalia, it was noted that the prophylactic rule set in *Miranda* was itself overprotective in that, by putting suspects on notice that they do not have to speak with police, "it sacrifices society's interest in uncovering evidence of crime and punishing those who violate its laws."[48] Society's interests in having an offender take responsibility for his actions are further sacrificed by the extensive practice of plea bargaining. [49]

While the most public element of an offender's post-arrest entanglement with the criminal justice system is a trial, approximately ninety-seven percent of criminal cases in the United States today are resolved by a plea of guilty.[50] In fact, the practice of plea bargaining has become so integral to the criminal justice system that but for its existence, the nation's crowded court system would suffer collapse.[51] Courts will accept and uphold a guilty plea so long as it is made "voluntarily and intelligently ... with adequate advice of counsel," and not provoked by "actual or threatened physical harm or by mental coercion overbearing the will of the defendant."[52] The government's interest in accepting a guilty plea is largely driven by efficiency, then, as guilty pleas avoid costly trials and often contain waivers of rights to appeal, while also obtaining a public admission of guilt from the offender.[53]

Though the argument can be made that a plea of guilty is an acceptance of responsibility, the overwhelming incentive for a defendant to plead guilty is the reward of a less severe sentence.[54] A common practice used by prosecutors to induce a defendant to engage in plea negotiations is to overcharge the offense committed.[55] Overcharging can drastically increase the potential for a long prison sentence.[56] As prosecutors are not constitutionally bound to turn over exculpatory evidence during the plea bargaining phase, they can often bluff as to the strength of their case, drastically reducing the bargaining power of the accused.[57] Defendants are often forced then, to choose between taking a deal to drastically reduce their sentence or face a trial where the odds appear daunting.[58] The result of these pressures is that accepting a guilty plea reduces a defendant's sentence by approximately two-thirds on average.[59] The risk of a lengthy prison term, often compounded by the practice of overcharging crimes, then, serves as a disincentive for telling the truth and taking full responsibility for one's actions.[60]

Little about the plea bargaining process, which is so pervasive and so heavily influences a defendant's criminal punishment, encourages offenders to take stock of their behavior or empathize with the victims of their actions.[61] When pleading guilty to a lesser included offense, an offender naturally fails to take full responsibility for the crime committed.[62] Simultaneously, offenders often feel coerced and victimized themselves by this system, which feeds into the alienation experienced between the offender and the community he has harmed.[63] This feeling of isolation from and victimization by society is only compounded by serving periods of incarceration designed mainly to punish and incapacitate an offender.

## 2. RECIDIVISM, POST-RELEASE EMPLOYMENT, AND COLLATERAL CONSEQUENCES

"Criminal capital formation," which argues that lengthier periods of incarceration lead directly to recidivism, is one of the leading theories on recidivism.[64] The theory's premise is that "inmates learn skills from their peers while incarcerated that make them more productive and active criminals upon release," essentially turning prisons into training camps for criminal behavior. [65] This phenomenon of negative peer learning, or "hardening," occurs naturally as inmates are kept in close quarters for long periods, with little positive societal influence.[66] In fact, of those offenders who are incarcerated a second time, nearly eighty percent will go on to be incarcerated repeatedly in the future.[67]

Another part of this argument that tends to show how longer prison sentences may lead to higher chances of recidivism is that the longer an individual is incapacitated, the lower that individual's chances become of finding meaningful employment once released.[68] According to the U.S. Attorney General's 2006 Report on Criminal History Background Checks, "steady gainful employment is a leading factor in preventing recidivism."[69] However, both private and public sector employers often exclude job applicants with criminal histories as a matter of policy.[70] It is not an uncommon practice for businesses to place advertisements for entry level job openings that specifically state something to the effect of: "Do not apply with any misdemeanors or felonies."[71] Even those offenders who are able to find a job work for lower than average wages.[72] And often, recently released offenders are severely handicapped financially by orders to pay restitution, court costs, court-appointed attorney's fees, and other fines.[73] Newly reintegrated offenders, then, are caught in a "Catch-22" situation, where their status as recently released puts them at the highest risk for recidivism, while also making them less likely to be hired for even a low-paying job.[74]

Aside from mere discrimination of convicts in employment, long term incarceration deprives an offender of experience and training in the modern workforce.[75] In Louisiana, for example, seventy-three percent of prison inmates receive no education or job training while incarcerated.[76] A cruel irony in the Louisiana system, however, is that inmates serving life sentences are able to become certified air conditioning technicians and welders, even though they will likely never ply their trades outside of prison walls.[77] In other prison systems, status as a "violent offender" precludes inmates from otherwise available prison work or job training opportunities.[78]

Released offenders who endured long-term incarceration also struggle with modern technology and even commonplace home appliances.[79] Some long-term incarcerated offenders walk out into the modern world suffering from "digital illiteracy," as they've had no experience using the internet or a smart phone.[80] Consequently, this lack of familiarity with technology means that some released offenders are forced to turn down potentially suitable employment simply because they struggle to fill out online job applications.[81] In addition to the practical barriers between themselves and gainful employment, offenders must also wrestle with the attachment of collateral consequences.

The moment a person is convicted of a felony, a plethora of collateral consequences attach.[82] Collateral consequences are legal or regulatory restrictions that prevent or limit a convicted offender's access to employment, occupational licensing, housing benefits, civil rights, and more.[83] The National Inventory of Collateral Consequences of Conviction reports more than 40,000 total consequences imposed by state, federal, and territorial law jurisdictions.[84] Some collateral consequences are offense-specific—such as requiring registration by sex offenders—but many apply without regard to the nature or severity of the convicted crime.[85] In most states, offenders with felony convictions face hundreds of barriers in the form of statutes, and administrative and state court rules, that make successful reintegration into the community onerous.[86] On average, a felony conviction in any given jurisdiction in the United States is accompanied by an average of seven hundred fifty collateral consequences, seventy-five percent of which directly impact employment opportunities.[87] Nearly 6,000 occupations require a license, and in many cases, a criminal conviction can function as a per se bar to licensure.[88] In many states, a criminal conviction can even bar an individual from employment involving low-level skill or training, such as being a barber or a nursing home aid.[89]

The net effect of employment discrimination against offenders, a lack of marketable job skills, and collateral consequences is that released offenders are often forced to choose between a minimum wage job—if they manage to get one—and highly lucrative criminal activity for which they received ample training while incarcerated.[90]

### 3. STIGMATIZATION & ISOLATION CONTRIBUTING TO RECIDIVISM

In addition to employment and collateral consequences of incarceration, stigmatization and isolation in society also contribute to recidivism. The stigmatization of offenders begins, for some, as early as being labeled a "delinquent" in the juvenile system.[91] For many offenders, especially at a young age, such a label effectively creates a self-fulfilling prophecy that they will continue to offend because they feel in some way already alienated from their communities.[92]

For adult offenders, the massive number of collateral consequences now permanently attached to them only reinforces alienation.[93] Collateral consequences are justified by some proponents on the theory that they are retributive criminal sanctions, whereas incarceration is a protective measure to incapacitate an offender from causing more harm.[94] However, if they are truly an effort to "set right the moral balance," collateral consequences should be proportional to the harm suffered.[95] Instead, the sheer number and reach of collateral consequences across so many jurisdictions is wildly over-inclusive, permanently denying the chance to ever "rejoin the moral order and reap the benefit of punishment."[96] In fact, the proliferation of legislative enactments "that emphasize the salience of the felon label exacerbate the permanence and severity of the mark of a criminal conviction."[97]

Naturally then, many offenders begin to see these restrictions on post-incarcerated life as an ongoing punishment, "promulgated by the State and spawned … to protect 'them' from 'us.'"[98] Among the assumptions that justify collateral consequences are the belief that criminal acts result from rotten character, that character—once demonstrated to be of the criminal nature—cannot be reformed, and that good character is necessary to function with all rights and privileges of citizens in society.[99] The legal framework for discriminating between the average citizen—people of "pure" character—and criminals—people with "blemished" character—only further reenforces the notion that once convicted, an offender is intrinsically "not quite human."[100] Offenders often internalize this message, further increasing the odds that they will not overcome the already daunting barriers in their path toward successful reintegration into the community.[101]

## b. Mass Incarceration's Effect on Communities

Once an individual is incarcerated, the effect caused by their absence in the community they leave behind can be well described as a ripple effect.[102] Two of the most important "ripples" are the effect of incarceration on an offender's children and community infrastructure.[103] Furthermore, because communities of color and economic disadvantage experience far higher rates of incarceration, its effects in those communities is compounded as "parent-aged adults, especially men, cycle through stays in prison and jail at astounding rates."[104]

The first major ripple effect of incarceration effects the children of offenders. Children of incarcerated parents are likely, if not guaranteed, to experience economic hardship, housing insecurity, and emotional and social isolation.[105] The fact that mothers dissolve relationships with male offenders who enter incarceration at extremely high levels inevitably further deteriorates the strained relationships between those offenders with their own children.[106] The effects of weakened emotional bonds are demonstrated by multiple studies showing that having a parent incarcerated is a risk factor for delinquency and "makes a child two and a half times more likely to develop a serious mental disorder."[107] Additionally, some studies suggest links between parental incarceration and later failures in school, chronic underemployment, and even drug use.[108]

The second major effect of incarceration involves a destabilization of a community's infrastructure. Communities with high incarceration rates experience increased economic instability, as families suddenly lose income earners while also being faced with additional expenses, such as lawyers, prison visits, and sending money to those incarcerated.[109] These economic adversities lead to more destabilization, crowded living conditions—as prisoners' families are often forced to move in with relatives for support—and changing school systems, which can negatively impact a child's performance in the classroom.[110] Mass incarceration effects the stability of communities by "raid[ing] supplies of local human capital and leav[ing] a gap in employable residents."[111] The cumulative effect of community destabilization manifests, among other ways, in higher rates of stress-related mental illness than the population at large.[112]

## c. The Effects of the Adversarial Process on Victims of Crime

The consequences of crime reach not only offenders and their communities, but they manifest in long term psychological and sometimes financial repercussions for victims as well. Because the system of prosecuting and sentencing focuses so heavily on punishing offenders, victims of crimes are often left suffering lasting effects not only as a result of the criminal act itself, but due to the process of justice and the outcome for the offender.[113] While efforts have been made in many jurisdictions to address the rights of victims, many barriers continue to exist that prevent victims from obtaining meaningful access to the justice system.[114] In fact, as one legal scholar noted, "the very notion of victims having some role to play in the system is mind-boggling to professionals in the system who cannot even envision where a victim might sit in the courtroom."[115]

### 1. NO MEANINGFUL OPPORTUNITY TO CONFRONT OFFENDER

The current criminal justice process does not provide a meaningful opportunity for victims of crime to confront offenders.[116] The American justice system has traditionally focused "on crime as a violation of the law, offering punishment as the appropriate remedy."[117] This largely retributive approach to justice and sentencing conveys that once a punishment has been handed down, "justice has been done."[118] Simply inflicting punishment from a top-down, macro-society level, however, cannot repair the harm done to victims and cannot "answer their questions, relieve their fears, help them make sense of their tragedy or help heal their wounds."[119] In this process, a victim's voice is hardly ever heard until they are confronted by their offender in the adversarial setting of the witness stand.[120]

In fact, an offender's Fifth Amendment rights under Confrontation Clause often cause continuing harm by placing victims in the position of defending themselves during rigorous cross-examination.[121]

Ethically, defense attorneys have a duty to represent the best interests of their clients, which often includes conducting vigorous cross-examination of witnesses.[122] Even where an attorney is aware that a victim is telling the truth, an attorney may ethically attempt to demonstrate that victim's bias against the defendant or destroy their credibility for truthfulness.[123] This is even true, though perhaps the question of ethics is more complex, when a cross-examiner knows the witness is telling the truth because of a confidential revelation by the offender.[124] Some attorneys may even toe the ethical line by being intentionally aggressive or even abusive in order to establish a reputation as a vigorous cross-examiner.[125] Victims of crime who experience ethically justifiable—or even mandatory—cross-examination may be left feeling as though their own suffering was used against them because the justice system considers the perpetrator's rights more highly than their own.[126]

Rape shield laws are one example of an area where the law has begun to recognize the negative psychological and reputational impact of certain types of cross-examination on victims.[127] These laws aim to diminish a defendant's ability to introduce evidence of a rape victim's prior sexual conduct with the aim of preventing a victim's unrelated sexual history from becoming a focal point of what is already an extremely difficult testimony emotionally.[128] While rape shield laws have attempted to protect the privacy of victims of sexual assault against certain types of cross-examination, some critics argue that these laws imply that women who are more sexually active are less deserving of the law's protection, which can further exacerbate a victim's psychological suffering.[129] A 1988 study focused on victims of sexual assault defined several common elements of "rape trauma syndrome," which include depression, anxiety, flashbacks, shame, and more.[130] These underlying conditions often manifest in behavior like social withdrawal, alcohol or drug abuse, and avoidance of "crime-related stimuli."[131]

## 2. CONTINUED PSYCHOLOGICAL EFFECTS OF VICTIMIZATION

However, the psychological effects of crime are not limited to victims of sexual assault.[132] In a study examining psychological ramifications of crime researchers found that "there was a general elevation on all consequences subscales," for victims of violent and non-violent crime alike.[133] While reporting that approximately fifty percent of violent crime victims experienced "moderate to extreme" levels of psychological distress, the study noted that the trauma experienced due to the crime seemed to effect a victim's sense of wellbeing more than merely the category of the crime.[134] Interestingly, victims of violent crime were significantly more likely to seek help from mental health services, which suggests that more resources are made available to victims of those kinds of crimes, even though victims of property or non-violent crimes may experience the same intensity of psychological trauma.[135]

Though the passage of time may alleviate the initial symptoms of trauma, victims of crime often experience long-term difficulty in returning to their "pre-victimization identity."[136] A victim's view of themselves or the world around them may be fundamentally altered by the traumatic experience endured at the hands of an offender.[137] Studies have shown that victims may internalize trauma which can manifest through continued anxiety about their personal safety, feelings of helplessness, low self-worth, or even inferiority, and isolation caused by a loss of trust in other people.[138] Essentially, "victimization alters the script [victims] follow in normal daily life."[139]

### 3. LACK OF RESTITUTION

Exacerbating the psychological distress suffered is the fact that crime victims are unlikely to be made whole financially. The movement toward making restitution payments available was certainly guided by the idea that "the loss to crime victims is recognized" in the justice system, and as such, was a positive step in the direction of victims' rights.[140] However, the issue of restitution raises not only Fifth and Sixth Amendment concerns for offenders, but also confusion among legal practitioners as to whether restitution is a criminal sentence or a civil award akin to damages.[141] The second issue matters to victims because the characterization of what restitution is defines the rights a victim maintains.[142] For example, in jurisdictions where courts have interpreted restitution as part of a criminal sentence, a victim of crime has no "authority to settle, release, satisfy, or otherwise modify a restitution judgment."[143] This interpretation once more sees victims of crime relegated to the sidelines in matters directly affecting their wellbeing.

Putting aside its more theoretical implications, victims of crime have practical problems being made financially whole as well. The United States Department of Justice even cautions victims that even though an offender may be ordered to pay restitution, "[r]ealistically … the chance of full recovery is very low."[144] As many times one offender may cause harm to numerous individuals, "restitution in the hundreds of thousands or millions of dollars is not unusual" in federal cases.[145] For those offenders who are able to pay, it is most likely that victims will receive payments in small amounts over a very long period of time.[146] Additionally, in federal cases, restitution orders are enforceable for only twenty years, meaning that an offender sentenced to long-term incarceration may only begin to make small payments by the time they are released, if they are released at all before the order expires.[147]

Even a willing offender's ability to pay restitution is severely hampered by the post-release economic conditions discussed above and the requirements that an offender's financial situation be taken into account when restitution is ordered. In one Tennessee case, for example, an offender convicted of burning a victim's personal property was ordered, joint and several with her co-defendants, to pay in excess of $94,000 in restitution in the amount of $150 per month.[148] Twelve years later, during a hearing for a probation violation, it was revealed that this single offender had paid nearly the entirety of what restitution payments had been made—nearly $25,000 to that point.[149] The judge, however, noted that at $150 per month, it would take the offender an additional twenty-nine years to pay the remaining balance, so he *sua sponte* ordered an effective doubling of her required annual restitution payments.[150] While this ruling would certainly have been helpful to restoring the crime's victims to their rightful position financially, the court of appeals reversed and remanded the decision because the trial judge failed to "consider the financial resources and future ability of the defendant to pay" as was required by statute.[151] The outcome of this case clearly demonstrates the ongoing disconnect between current retributive sentencing policy, an offender who is willing to accept responsibility, and the needs of victims to be made whole.

## PART III: RESTORATIVE JUSTICE AND ITS POTENTIAL TO DECREASE INCARCERATION WHILE OFFERING VICTIMS OF CRIME AND COMMUNITIES A SEAT AT THE TABLE

If then, the current system discourages offenders from taking responsibility for their actions, sets them up for long-term isolation and recidivism, destroys communities, and does little to foster healing for victims of crime, questions about whether that system should be altered to better serve the needs of all involved should be asked. Many aspects of restorative justice philosophy could be infused into the current system to address the needs of all interested parties. While not many restorative justice practices have been widely incorporated into the American criminal justice system, its potential to positively impact both offenders and victims of crime should not be judged against a perfect system, but rather, against "the deeply-flawed status quo."[152] Restorative justice practices will not be appropriate for every offender, nor will they be desired by every victim. That should not, however, deter us from an honest exploration of how these alternatives might function to reduce the long-term impacts of crime on all interested parties by fostering a sense of connectedness that can lead to the types of healing that are nearly unfathomable in the current system.

This section will seek to further define restorative justice philosophy and to discuss why it should be incorporated into the sentencing system, in view of its potential to reduce recidivism for offenders, address the needs of victims, and foster reintegration into the community for both.

## a. What Restorative Justice is

Howard Zehr, who directed the first victim-offender conferencing program in the United States, calls restorative justice "an approach to achieving justice that involves, to the extent possible, those who have a stake in a specific offense or harm to collectively identify and address harms, needs, and obligations in order to heal and put things as right as possible."[153] The three main goals of restorative justice philosophy are to reduce the likelihood that an offender will recidivate, to put key decisions in the hands of victims of crime, and to offer a view of justice that fosters both accountability and healing.[154] In practice, these goals require first that offenders understand how their actions have harmed other people and are willing to take responsibility for those actions. Second, victims of crime must be involved in the process of justice, having a say in how the harms suffered are repaired. Lastly, offenders and victims can be reintegrated into the community, granting a sense of closure and connectedness.[155]

## 1. WHAT RESTORATIVE JUSTICE IS NOT

Before delving into the form restorative justice practices may take to achieve these aims, it may be helpful to note some things that restorative justice is not. First and foremost, restorative justice is not a replacement for the legal system.[156] Most advocates of these practices acknowledge that crime has both public and intra-personal dimensions, and that the government's interest in societal order through prosecuting crime must be not overlooked.[157] The aim of restorative justice would not be to occupy the place of the legal system, but to work in connection with it, keeping both prosecutors and judges involved in the outcomes.[158] In practice, restorative programs would offer a more balanced approach to the issue of addressing societal harms and intra-personal harms together.[159]

Next, restorative justice practices are not necessarily alternatives to prison.[160] Proponents of restorative justice acknowledge that there are simply cases where retributive punishment or incapacitation are necessary to prevent further harm, and there are also cases where it may be appropriate to use restorative practices in conjunction with prison sentences.[161] However, accomplishing the goals of restorative practices would certainly reduce the legal system's reliance on retributive incarceration, thus reducing the overall prison population and the risk of recidivism.[162]

Additionally, restorative justice should not be seen as primarily trying to achieve forgiveness or reconciliation between offenders and victims.[163] The goal of restorative programs is not to encourage or coerce victims of crimes into forgiving offenders, but rather, to provide victims greater access to the justice system in order to aid in healing the traumas of crime.[164] In line with this goal is the requirement that participation in any restorative program must be voluntary—no victim should ever be forced to confront an offender.[165] In addition, a prerequisite for participation on the part of the offender is some kind of acknowledgment of the harm caused and his or her responsibility for that harm.[166] While not focusing primarily on achieving forgiveness or reconciliation, a potential benefit of restorative practices is that they would provide a context where forgiveness and reconciliation could occur, offering greater healing for all parties.[167]

Lastly, restorative justice is not a particular program or blueprint, but rather a set of principles applied to evolving and flexible practices.[168] Rather than viewing restorative justice as a map, Howard Zehr argues that it should be viewed "as a compass offering direction."[169] This means that restorative programs should be built from the community level, with an acknowledgement that they will be, to some degree, culture specific.[170] Allowing for flexibility among models from one community to the next, rather than imposing a "top down" model, furthers the aim of giving voice to victims and communities who are harmed.[171]

## 2. RESTORATIVE JUSTICE MODELS IN PRACTICE

As a result of the aim that restorative justice practices should be flexible, many various models have developed, including victim-offender mediations, family or community group conferences, circles, and video letters.[172] Many proponents envision a system where referrals to restorative programs would come from within the court system, either in the form of diversionary programs or in consideration for sentencing after a case has been decided.[173] In some models, a court-appointed mediator would receive a referral, evaluate whether some restorative practice may be appropriate—assessing the nature of the crime, the age or background of the participants, and the likelihood that they will interact with each other in the future, among other factors—and then contact the interested parties.[174] If the parties are willing, the mediator can recommend specific programs based on the parties' needs and desired outcomes.[175]

The programs offered would be moderated by a specifically trained facilitator.[176] The facilitator would be charged with developing a plan in consultation with the parties that addresses both the harm caused and what potential outcomes could be reached.[177] In cooperation with a victim, the facilitator could offer a "surrogate" encounter, for instance, where the victim is paired with a surrogate offender who caused a similar harm, thereby eliminating any trauma that could be caused by a direct face-to-face encounter.[178] Where a direct face-to-face encounter is not possible or desirable, other practices offered can include letter writing or video exchanges.[179] The aim of these encounters is again, to allow the parties to "humanize" each other by being mutually and respectfully heard.[180] It is in these encounters where the harm caused and the remedy to be achieved are taken into account that restorative justice proponents contend that healing can occur which allows both offenders and victims a path toward reintegration in their communities.[181]

### b. Offenders and Restorative Justice

While not necessarily established on a large scale, restorative justice programs have been shown to reduce recidivism rates of offenders.[182] When used as a diversionary tool, restorative programs can keep offenders out of the prison population, thus reducing not only the sheer number of those incarcerated, but also reducing the risk of recidivism that accompanies a prison sentence.[183] Offenders who participate in some form of victim-offender mediation are less likely to recidivate because, "once an offender has had an opportunity to meet the victim it becomes more difficult to rationalize committing such crime in the future."[184] Restorative programs may also help serve to shield offenders from the attachment of collateral consequences and the stigma of being incarcerated by offering a path to reentry into the community.[185] And by focusing on humanizing victims of crime and offering offenders the opportunity to take responsibility for their actions outside of the mainly retributive criminal justice system, offenders tend to feel less isolated from society and less abused by the system.[186]

The effect of restorative justice practices on offenders has been demonstrated in several studies to produce lower recidivism rates.[187] A study out of Campbell University's Norman Adrian Wiggins School of Law saw a reduction in the recidivism rate between sixteen and twenty-four percent where offenders participated in face-to-face mediation with victims.[188] One restorative program in Indianapolis which offers family group conferences, where juvenile offenders and their families meet the victims of their crime, has resulted "in a significant reduction in recidivism among these offenders."[189] Another study out of the United Kingdom demonstrated a recidivism rate just over fifteen percent for offenders who participated in face-to-face mediation, compared to a rate of nearly twenty-two percent for offenders who did not participate.[190] In contrast to face-to-face meetings, a two-year study by an outside consultant at the Healing and Sentencing Program at Whitehorse, Yukon Territory showed an eighty percent decrease in recidivism for offenders who participated in facilitated circles.[191] While again, there is perhaps no definitive, large-scale study that has conclusively demonstrated the exact potential for reductions in recidivism, at the very least, more than thirty studies have shown no increase in recidivism where restorative practices are used.[192] While additional research in this area is certainly welcomed, the data does show promise in the area of reducing recidivism and encouraging community reintegration among offenders who participate in restorative programs.

## c. Crime Victims and Restorative Justice

Perhaps the greatest potential for restorative justice practices, however, lies in their ability to offer victims of crime better access to the justice system and a path toward healing. Legal scholarship has recognized for some years that "a full appreciation of the rights of crime victims requires a 'third model' that does not fit comfortably with the existing prosecution- and defendant-oriented paradigms" within the current system.[193] Rather than putting victims on the stand in an adversarial proceeding or shutting out their voice completely, restorative programs allow crime victims to ask questions about the incident, express their feelings, and contribute to what it means to have a meaningful resolution of the case.[194] Many surveys of victims of crime indicate that they often "prefer a justice system focused on rehabilitation over punishment…and believe that prison is more likely to make people commit crimes," which means that a victim's desire for a specific type of justice is completely disregarded in a purely retributive scheme.[195]

Restorative practices, on the other hand, offer victims the opportunity to be meaningfully heard and have a voice in the justice process, helping to overcome feelings of isolation and powerlessness.[196] An additional benefit to restorative practices may be in providing a similar sense of closure in the many cases where a crime victim's offender is never apprehended.[197] These types of victims are often left feeling completely excluded from the justice process at all, and restorative practices such as victim circles or surrogate offender meetings could offer those victims healing through community support, the act of having their voice heard, and the humanization of a similarly situated offender.[198]

Considering the aim of better outcomes for victims of crime, numerous randomized control studies have demonstrated "that restorative justice outperformed the criminal process on a variety of metrics related to victims' psychological wellbeing and sense of fairness."[199] A randomized, multi-year study in Australia showed that "victims of violent crime who went to court were five times more likely to believe they would be revictimized by the offender than victims whose cases were referred to restorative justice."[200] This same study found that those "victims who participated in a restorative conference felt more secure, less anxious, less afraid of the offender, and had a greater sense of closure than those whose cases were resolved in the criminal process."[201] In a separate study the percentage of victims who felt either "quite" or "very" angry fell from sixty percent to thirty percent after those victims participated in restorative conferences.[202] At the same time, "the proportion of victims feeling sympathetic to the offender almost doubled."[203] Additionally, research in South Australia among juvenile offenders involving family conferences concluded that nine out of ten victims not only found the conferences helpful, but said they would attend again if they were ever victimized again.[204] The data shows that restorative justice programs may offer that "third model" that can more effectively appreciate the needs of victims than the current retributive justice system.[205]

### d. Communities and Restorative Justice

In addition to offering benefits to offenders and victims of crime, restorative justice programs offer a more productive system in which power is redistributed to the community level to redress the harms caused by crime.[206] In keeping with its holistic view of harm, restorative justice acknowledges that whole communities are often implicated in the harms caused by crime, and seeks to aid both victim and offender by engaging the relevant community in offering support or repairing the harm.[207] Further, and consistent with the idea that restorative practices should remain flexible, representation of the community may look different depending on the scenario.[208] The relevant community may be a workplace or school where the harm occurred, or it may simply involve family members, neighbors, or friends of the interested parties.[209] In other, larger-scale cases, the relevant community may be members of a particular religious or ethnic group.[210]

In either situation, restorative justice seeks to engage relevant communities in the justice process by calling on them "to leverage relationships and social networks in churches, neighborhood groups, and schools," to repair the harm.[211] Rather than relying on the current "top-down" retributive system, which has decimated entire communities through mass incarceration, restorative justice again seeks to redress the harms caused by crime in the places where those affected by it are found.[212] Community involvement in restorative practices reinforces social bonds, "help[ing] people stay connected to their communities and prevent crimes of self-interest."[213] When offenders do commit crimes, restorative practices allow for the "repairing of relationships and encouraging empathy," building on established social bonds in order to foster reintegration and to "undermine the cycles of poverty and crime."[214]

In addition to its potential to repair relationships and foster community accountability, restorative justice models can potentially mitigate racial and economic disparities within the current system of retributive mass incarceration.[215] The current level of government spending on law enforcement, the judiciary, and corrections equates to a per capita cost of $872 per year for every American.[216] In addition to achieving higher satisfaction rates among victims and offenders, restorative justice programs were shown in a series of thirty-six direct comparison cases to have "reduced costs associated with the criminal justice process as well as subsequent costs associated with the treatment of victim trauma."[217] There is a case to be made, then, that the widespread implementation of restorative practices could allow government to reinvest money from the current retributive incarceration system back into the communities most affected by crime, thus reducing the unequal impacts of punishment.[218]

# CONCLUSION

There is no amount of sheer punishment meted out to an offender that can make a victim of crime feel whole. While the current retributive sentencing structure leaves victims out in the cold, feeling as though their needs and desires are completely unheard, it also stigmatizes offenders, lining their path to reintegration into the community with numerous and nearly insurmountable barriers. Where the current system of retributive sentencing fails to meet the needs of victims of crime, offenders, and the communities where crime occurs, better options should be explored.

Restorative justice is an evolving philosophy that does not claim perfection, but certainly offers hope of a more redemptive system of sentencing and dealing with the consequences of crime on all parties who feel its effects. Integrating restorative justice practices into a larger sentencing scheme would offer victims of crime a seat at the table, allowing their voices to be heard and the potential for healing. Such practices would also give offenders the incentive to understand the harms caused by their actions in human terms and grant the willing among them the opportunity to make amends to the extent possible. This outcome in and of itself would keep many offenders out of the mass incarceration system, thereby reducing the risk of recidivism. Finally, a sentencing structure which incorporates restorative justice has the potential to repair communities devastated by the effects of retributive sentencing, while at the same time reducing inequalities and allowing communities a voice in what justice should look like and how to support the reintegration of all parties affected by crime.

# ENDNOTES

1    Howard Zehr, *The Little Book of Restorative Justice* 21 (2015).

2    Adriaan Lanni, *Article: Taking Restorative Justice Seriously*, 69 Buffalo L. Rev. 635, 643 (2021).

3    Ed Cameron, *Symposium: Some Psychoanalytic Aspects of Serial Homicide*, 24 Cardozo L. Rev. 2267, 2272 (2003).

4    Zehr, *supra* at 21, 24.

5    Dr. James Austin, *A Guidelines Proposal: How Many Americans are Unnecessarily Incarcerated?*, 29 Fed. Sent. R. 140 (2017).

6    James M. Binnall, *Article: EG1900 … The Number they Gave me When they Revoked my Citizenship: Perverse Consequences of Ex-Felon Civic Exile*, 44 Willamette L. Rev. 667, 688 (2008).

7    *Id.* at 668.

8    Joanna Shepherd, *Article: Blakely's Silver Lining: Sentencing Guidelines, Judicial Discretion, and Crime*, 58 Hastings L.J. 533, 547-48 (2007).

9    Zehr, *supra* at 7.

10   Alyssa H. Shenk, *Note: Victim-Offender Mediation: The Road to Repairing Hate Crime Injustice*, 17 Ohio St. J. on Disp. Resol. 185, 188-89 (2001).

11   Lanni, *supra* at 640-41.

12   Zehr, *supra* at 31-34.

13   Shenk, *supra* at 189.

14   Zehr, *supra* at 48.

15   Lara Bazelon, *Rectify* 134 (2018).

16 Zehr, *supra* at 29.

17 *Id.* at 32-33.

18 Bazelon, *supra* at 5.

19 Lanni, *supra* at 637.

20 *Id.* at 637, 644.

21 *Id.* at 638.

22 *Id.* at 642.

23 Andrew D. Leipold, *Article: Is Mass Incarceration Inevitable?*, 56 Am. Crim. L. Rev. 1579, 1580 (2019).

24 *Id.* at 1580.

25 Austin, *supra*.

26 *Id.*

27 *Id.*

28 Shannon M. Silva, Elizabeth H. Porter-Merrill, and Pete Lee, *Article: Fulfilling the Aspirations of Restorative Justice in the Criminal System? The Case of Colorado*, 28 Kan. J.L. & Pub. Pol'y 456, 457 (2019).

29 Austin, *supra*.

30 *Id.*

31 Oliver Roeder, et al., *What Caused the Crime Decline*, Brennan Ctr. for Justice, https://www.brennancenter.org/publication/what-caused-crime-decline

32 Austin, *supra*.

33 Roeder, *supra*.

34 Roeder, *supra*.

35 Roeder, *supra*.

36 Austin, *supra*.

37 *Id.*

38   *Length of Incarceration and Recidivism,* United States Sentencing Commission (2020), https://www.ussc.gov/sites/default/files/pdf/research-and-publications/research-publications/2020/20200429_Recidivism-SentLength.pdf

39   Shira E. Gordon, *Note: Solitary Confinement, Public Safety, and Recidivism,* 47 U. Mich. J.L. Reform 495, 516-17 (2014).

40   Austin, *supra.*

41   Gordon, *supra* at 519.

42   United States Sentencing Commission, *supra.*

43   Carolyn W. Deady, *Incarceration and Recidivism: Lessons from Abroad,* Pell Center for International Relations and Public Policy (2014), http://www.antoniocasella.eu/nume/Deady_march2014.pdf

44   Zehr, *supra* at 75.

45   *Miranda v. Arizona,* 384 U.S. 436, 469 (1966).

46   *Duckworth v. Eagan,* 492 U.S. 195, 202 (1989).

47   *Miranda,* 384 U.S. 467-68.

48   *Duckworth,* 492 U.S. 209.

49   Zehr, *supra* at 24.

50   Andrew M. Pardieck, Vanessa A. Edkins, and Lucian E. Dervan, *Article: Bargained Justice: The Rise of False Testimony for False Please,* 44 Fordham Int'l L.J. 469, 482 (2020).

51   *Id.* at 481.

52   *Id.* at 482.

53   Daniel P. Blank, *Article: Plea Bargaining Wavers Reconsidered: A Legal Pragmatist's Guide to Loss, Abandonment and Alienation,* 68 Fordham L. Rev. 2011, 2077 (2000).

54   Tziporah Schwartz Tapp, *Recent Development: Refusing to Compare Apples and Oranges: Why the Fourth Circuit Got it Right in United States v. Divens,* 90 N.C.L. Rev. 1267, 1289 (2012).

55   Blank, *supra* at 2041.

56  *Id.*

57  *Id.* at 2040.

58  *Id.* at 2031.

59  Jon'a F. Meyer, *Plea Bargaining*, Britannica. https://www.britannica.com/topic/plea-bargaining (last modified February 16, 2020).

60  Zehr, *supra* at 24.

61  *Id.*

62  *Id.*

63  *Id.*

64  David S. Abrams, *Article: The Imprisoner's Dilemma: A Cost-Benefit Approach to Incarceration*, 98 Iowa L. Rev. 905, 917 (2013).

65  *Id.*

66  Miguel F.P. de Figueiredo, *Article: Throw Away the Key or Throw Away the Jail? The Effect of Punishment on Recidivism and Social Cost*, 47 Ariz. St. L.J. 1017, 1022 (2015).

67  Todd R. Clear (ed. By Michael Tonry), *Article: The Effects of High Imprisonment Rates on Communities*, 37 Crime & Just. 97, 98 (2008).

68  Abrams, *supra* at 950-51.

69  Office of the Att'y Gen., U.S. Dep't of Justice, *The Attorney General's Report on Criminal History Background Checks* 2 (2006).

70  Shristi Devu, *Comments: Trapped in the Shackles of America's Criminal Justice System*, 20 Scholar 217, 226-27 (2018).

71  *Id.* at 227.

72  Stacy A. Hickox, Article: A Call to Reform State Restrictions on Hiring of Ex-Offenders, 12 Stan. J.C.R. & C.L. 121, 124 (2016).

73  Courtney Harper Turkington, *Comment: Louisiana's Addiction to Mass Incarceration by the Numbers*, 63 Loy. L. Rev. 557, 572 (2017).

74  Robert Blecker, *Article: Haven or Hell? Inside Lorton Central Prison: Experiences of Punishment Justified.*, 42 Stan. L. Rev. 1149, 1198 (1990).

75   Shepherd, *supra* at 547.

76   Turkington, *supra:* at 572.

77   *Id.*at 571-72.

78   Michael O'Hear, *Criminal Law: Third-Class Citizenship: The Escalating Legal Consequences of Committing a "Violent" Crime*, 109 J. Crim. L. & Criminology 165, *196.

79   Leslie Scott, *Article: "It Never, Ever Ends": The Psychological Impact of Wrongful Convictions*, 5 Crim. L. Brief 10, 15 (2010).

80   Alexandra Marquez, *Former prisoners struggle to re-enter society: What happens when society moves online?*, NBC News (Mar. 28, 2021) https://www.nbcnews.com/tech/tech-news/former-prisoners-struggle-re-enter-society-happens-society-moves-onlin-rcna518

81   Gail L. Heriot, *Article: Title VII Disparate Impact Liability Makes Almost Everything Presumptively Illegal*, 14 NYU J.L & Liberty 1, 35 (2020).

82   Michael Pinard, *Article: An Integrated Perspective on the Collateral Consequences of Criminal Convictions and Reentry Issues Faced by Formerly Incarcerated Individuals*, 86 B.U.L. Rev. 623, 630 (2006).

83   *What are Collateral Consequences?* National Inventory of Collateral Consequences of Conviction. https://niccc.nationalreentryresourcecenter.org/ (last visited Nov. 21, 2021).

84   *After the Sentence, More Consequences: A National Snapshot of Barriers to Work.* National Inventory of Collateral Consequences of Conviction (2021), https://csgjusticecenter.org/publications/after-the-sentence-more-consequences/national-snapshot/

85   National Inventory of Collateral Consequences of Conviction, *supra*.

86   Devu, *supra* at 226.

87   National Inventory of Collateral Consequences of Conviction, *supra*.

88   Hickox, *supra* at 151.

89   *Id.*

90   Shepherd, *supra* at 547-48.

91   Gordon, *supra* at 518.

92   *Id.*

93   Binnall, *supra Article EG1900* ... at 668.

94   *Id.*at 677.

95   *Id.*

96   *Id.*at 679.

97   James M. Binnall, *Article: Sixteen Million Angry Men: Reviving a Dead Doctrine to Challenge the Constitutionality of Excluding Felons from Jury Service*, 17 Va. J. Soc. Pol'y & L. 1, 26 (2009).

98   Binnall, *supra Article EG1900* ... at 668.

99   *Id.*at 671.

100  *Id.*at 680.

101  *Id.*at 688.

102  Clear, *supra* at 98-99.

103  *Id.* at 99.

104  *Id.* at 100-02.

105  *Id.*at 103-05.

106  *Id.*at 112.

107  *Id.* at 110.

108  *Id.*

109  *Id.*at 112.

110  *Id.*at 112-13.

111  *Id.*at 115-16.

112  Silva, *supra* at 457.

113  Zehr, *supra* at 21.

114  Paul G. Cassell, *Symposium: Barbarians at the Gates? A Reply to the Critics of the Victims' Rights Amendment*, 1999 Utah L. Rev. 479, 481 (1999).

115  *Id.*

116  Zehr, *supra* at 21.

117  Shenk, *supra* at 189.

118  *Id.*

119  *Id.* at 185.

120  R. George Wright, *Article: Cross-Examining Legal Ethics: The Roles of Intentions, Outcomes, and Character*, 83 Ky. L.J. 801, 808-09 (1995).

121  *Id.* at 802.

122  *Id.* at 802-03.

123  *Id.*

124  *Id.* at 803.

125  *Id.* at 802.

126  Zehr, *supra* at 21.

127  I. Bennett Capers, *Article: Real Women, Real Rape*, 60 UCLA L. Rev. 826, 828 (2013).

128  *Id.*

129  *Id.* at 828-29 (2013).

130  James K. Hill, Ph.D., *Victims' Response to Trauma and Implications for Interventions: A Selected Review and Synthesis of the Literature*, Department of Justice of Canada, Policy Centre for Victims Issues, Research and Statistics Division 5 (2003), https://www.justice.gc.ca/eng/rp-pr/cj-jp/victim/rr03_vic2/rr03_vic2.pdf

131  *Id.*

132  *Id.* at 6.

133  *Id.*

134  *Id.*

135  *Id.* at 7.

136 *Id.*

137 *Id.* at 6.

138 *Id.*

139 *Id.*

140 David Peters, *Comment: Unsettled: Victim Discretion in the Administration of Criminal Restitution Orders*, 166 U. Pa. L. Rev. 1293, 1289 (2018).

141 *Id.* at 1300.

142 *Id. at 1300-01.*

143 *Id.* at 1301.

144 *Restitution Process*, The United States Department of Justice, Criminal Division, Victim Notification Program (last visited Nov. 21, 2021) https://www.justice.gov/criminal-vns/restitution-process

145 *Id.*

146 *Id.*

147 *Id.*

148 *State v. Petty*, 2021 Tenn. Crim. App. LEXIS 181, *1-2 (Tenn. Ct. App.).

149 *Id.* at *5.

150 *Id.* at *5-6.

151 *Id.* at *10-12.

152 Lanni, *supra* at 638.

153 Zehr, *supra* at 48.

154 *Id.*

155 *Id.* at 48-49.

156 *Id.* at 19.

157 *Id.*

158 *Id.* at 58.

159 *Id.* at 19-20.

160 *Id.* at 20.

161 *Id.*

162 *Id.*

163 *Id.* at 13.

164 *Id.*

165 Jennifer L. Kerrigan, *Comment: "It's Not World Peace, But…" Restorative Justice: Analysis of Recidivism Rates in Campbell Law School's Juvenile Justice Project*, 30 Campbell L. Rev. 339, 346 (2008).

166 Zehr, *supra* at 57-58.

167 *Id.* at 13.

168 *Id.* at 16-17.

169 *Id.* at 17.

170 *Id.*

171 *Id.*

172 Kerrigan, *supra* at 342-43.

173 Zehr, *supra* at 58.

174 Kerrigan, *supra* at 346-47.

175 *Id.* at 346.

176 Zehr, *supra* at 61.

177 *Id.* at 62.

178 *Id.* at 67.

179 *Id.* at 37.

180 Kerrigan, *supra* at 348.

181 Zehr, *supra* at 48-49.

182  *Id.* at 16.

183  Lanni, *supra* at 637.

184  Shenk, *supra* at 215.

185  *Id.*at 646.

186  Lanni, *supra* at 645-46.

187  Kerrigan, *supra* at 357.

188  *Id.*

189  Mark S. Umbreit, Betty Vos, Robert B. Coates, and Elizabeth Lightfoot, *Article: Restorative Justice: An Empirically Grounded Movement Facing Many Opportunities and Pitfalls*, 8 Cardozo J. Conflict Resol. 511, 524 (2007).

190  *Id.* at 545.

191  *Id.* at 548.

192  John Braithwaite, *Article: Restorative Justice: Assessing Optimistic and Pessimistic Accounts*, 25 Crime & Just. 1, 35 (1999).

193  Cassell, *supra* at 481.

194  Lanni, *supra* at 643.

195  *Id.*

196  *Id.*

197  Umbreit, *supra* at 563.

198  Shepherd, *supra* at 190-91.

199  Lanni, *Supra* at 644.

200  *Id.*

201  *Id.*

202  Braithwaite, *supra* at 24.

203  *Id.*

204  *Id.* at 24-24.

205 Cassell, *supra* at 481.

206 Silva, *supra* at 471.

207 *Id.*

208 *Id.*

209 *Id.*

210 *Id.*

211 *Id.*at 472-73.

212 *Id.*

213 *Id.*at 473.

214 *Id.*

215 *Id.*at 476-77.

216 *Id.*at 475.

217 *Id.*

218 *Id.*at 476.

# ABOUT THE AUTHOR

Brandon Dragan grew up in northeastern New Jersey and attended Belmont University in Nashville, Tennessee. He is currently a 3L Juris Doctor candidate at Belmont University College of Law.

Brandon enjoys road cycling, cigars, Irish whisky, and is an avid supporter of the Arsenal Football Club. He and his wife Jami live in the Nashville area with their two daughters.

For more information, visit:
BrandonDragan.com

**Many voices. One message.**

Quoir is a boutique publisher that provides
concept-to-publication solutions and creative services for print
and digital books, podcasts, and videos. We are committed to
being author-centric, collaborative, and unconventional.
For more information, please visit
*www.quoir.com*

CPSIA information can be obtained
at www.ICGtesting.com
Printed in the USA
BVHW030014210322
631966BV00001B/13

9 781957 007106